D1518312

THE MANY LOVES OF DOBIE GILLIS

eleven campus stories

BY MAX SHULMAN

ÆONIAN PRESS

MATTITUCK

Reprinted 1976 by Special Arrangement

International Standard Book Number 0-89190-982-6

To the Reader

It is our pleasure to keep available uncom-
mon fiction and to this end, at the time of
publication, we have used the best available
sources. To aid catalogers and collectors,
this title is printed in an edition limited to 300
copies.   ——— Enjoy!

To order contact
AEONIAN PRESS, INC.
Box 1200
Mattituck, New York 11952

to

FERDINAND DE LESSEPS

without whom I never could have dug the Suez Canal

Contents

Contents

The Unlucky
Winner

My next girl is going to be honest. I don't care if she looks like a doorknob. Just so she's honest.

This determination arises from a late unhappy attachment to one Clothilde Ellingboe. Now, don't misunderstand; I'm not calling Clothilde a crook. Let's say she was irresponsible. Or unethical. Or unprincipled. Or amoral. Let's not go around calling ladies crooks. Watch that stuff.

I met Clothilde at the University of Minnesota's annual Freshman Prom. I was standing in the stag line and I saw her dancing with a fellow halfway across the floor. They were doing the "Airborne Samba," the latest dance craze at the university. In the "Airborne Samba" the girl locks her hands behind the fellow's neck and he carries her all through the dance. She never touches the floor; she just lashes out rhythmically with her feet.

I cut in on them, laughing lightly at the resultant abrasions. I transported Clothilde through the rest of the medley, and then we went out on the terrace for some air. There, in a very short time, I knew I was hers. How vivacious she was! How socially aware she was! You would never believe she was only a freshman, the way she had been everywhere and had done everything and knew everyone. In a very short time I was, as I say, hers.

Then began a social whirl that I would not have thought possible. We were out every night—dancing, movies, sleigh rides, hayrides, wiener roasts, bridge games, community sings. Not a night did we miss.

At first I was a little worried. "Clothilde," I would say, "I'd love to go out tonight, but I've got homework. I've got to translate ten pages of Virgil for Latin tomorrow."

"Dobie, you oaf," she would laugh. "Don't you know *anything?*"

Then she would produce a Virgil pony—a Latin textbook with English translations set in smaller type beneath each line of Latin.

When I said that I had to do some work in political science, she would hand me a syllabus that condensed the whole course into an hour's easy reading. If I was concerned about an English history quiz, she would come up with a card the size of a bookmark on which there was printed the dates of all the kings in the British dynasty, plus thumbnails of all significant events.

"This is all very well," I said one night, "but I don't feel that I'm learning anything."

"To the contrary, Dobie," she replied, taking my hands in hers. "Without all this social life, you could never become a well-rounded-out personality. What's more important, Dobie—to know a lot of old facts and figures or to become a well-rounded-out personality?"

"To become a well-rounded-out personality," I said. "Clearly."

"There you are," she said, spreading her palms. "C'mon, Dobie, let's go down to the Kozy Kampus Kave and hear E-String Eddie and his T.N.T. Trio."

And so it went, night after night. I'll confess that I was a stranger to the Phi Beta Kappa selection board, but nonetheless, my grades were adequate. I got by, and whatever happened in my classes, I had the comfort of knowing that I was becoming a well-rounded-out personality. Some

nights I could actually feel my personality rounding out—like a balloon.

But occasionally a doubt would dart through my mind like a lizard across a rock. Then I would say to myself, "This can't go on forever." I found out I was right one morning in my English class.

On that morning at the end of the class hour, our instructor, Mr. Hambrick, announced, "There will be a five-hundred-word theme due next Friday. Write about any subject you want to. No excuses will be accepted for late themes. Class dismissed."

The heart within me sank. I had long been worried about Mr. Hambrick. Mr. Hambrick was one of those college English instructors who had taken a teaching job thirty years before so they could have an income while they worked on their novels. Now they were still teaching English and they were still on the first chapters of their novels. They vented their frustration on their students.

Up to this assignment I had managed to get along in Mr. Hambrick's class. Before this I had had to turn in three or four book reports, all of which Clothilde supplied from the *Book Review Digest*. But a theme was different. You can't go about clipping original themes from other sources.

"Clothilde," I said that evening, "I'm afraid the movies are out for tonight. I've got to turn in a theme for English on Friday and here it is Tuesday and I'd better get to work."

"But, Dobie," wailed Clothilde. "It's Montgomery Clift. He knocks me out. Doesn't he knock you out?"

"No," I said truthfully. "Listen, Clothilde, I'd better do this theme. This isn't the kind of thing I can chisel on. I've got to do it myself, and I'd better get started."

"How long does it have to be?"

"Five hundred words."

"What's the topic?"

"Anything I want."

"Well, then, what's your hurry? It's only Tuesday. You've got Wednesday and Thursday to work on it."

"No, I'd better start it right away. I don't know whether I can finish it all in one night. Don't forget, Clothilde, I'm not very bright."

"Yes, I know," she said, "but even *you* should be able to write a five-hundred-word theme in one night. Especially if you can pick your own subject."

"Look, Clothilde, I don't want to seem stubborn, but I've made up my mind. I'm going to start that theme tonight and that's final."

"Shelly Winters is in the picture too."

"Let's hurry so we can get good seats," I said.

The next night, Wednesday, I was positively going to work on the theme. *Positively.* But Benny Goodman was playing a one-night stand at the Auditorium, and, as Clothilde said, "You can't just not go to hear Benny Goodman. How will you explain it to people?"

And Thursday afternoon there was a Sunlite Dance in the Union with a jitterbug contest for which Clothilde and I had been rehearsing for weeks. Unfortunately, Clothilde threw a shoe and pulled up lame at the end of the second lap and we had to drop out.

Not until six o'clock Thursday evening did I get to the theme. I set two fountain pens, a bottle of ink, an eraser, three pencils, a dictionary, a thesaurus, and a ream of fresh white paper on my desk. I adjusted the goose-neck lamp for minimum eyestrain. I pulled up a straight-back chair. I opened the window. I filled a pitcher with water, I took my phone off the hook. Then I sat down and drew isosceles triangles for two hours.

Not an idea came to me. Not a fragment of an idea. Not a teensy-weensy glimmer of an idea. I had just about decided to drop out of the university and enroll in a manual-training school when I heard Clothilde calling me outside my window.

I stuck my head out. "How ya doin', Dobie?" she asked.

I grimaced.

"I thought so," she said. "Well, don't worry. I've got it all figured out. Look." She held up two white cards.

"What's that?" I asked.

"Stack permits," she replied.

"What?"

"Come on out and I'll explain the whole thing."

"Listen, Clothilde, I don't know what you're up to, but I don't want any part of it. I'm going to sit here all night if I have to, but I'm going to finish that theme. I don't care what you say; there's no other way to do it."

"Come on out, you jerk. I've never failed you yet, have I? Listen, you'll not only have your theme written tonight, but we'll be able to catch the last feature at the Bijou."

"No."

"You don't really believe you're going to get that theme written, do you?"

She had me there.

"Come on out."

"What's a stack permit?" I asked.

"Come on out."

I came out.

She took my arm. "We'd better hurry, Dobie. It's after eight o'clock and the library closes at nine."

"What's that got to do with anything?"

She was pulling me along, toward the library. "Dobie, you've been to the library, haven't you?"

"I used to go occasionally," I said, "before I met you."

"All right. You know how the library works?"

"Sure," I said. "You go in and look up the book you want in the card catalogue and then you write your name and the card number of the book on a request slip and you give the slip to the librarian and she sends a page boy after your book."

"Ah," said Clothilde, "but do you know where the books come from?"

"They keep them on shelves in the back of the library."

"Stacks," said Clothilde. "Those are called stacks."

"So?"

"Ordinarily," Clothilde continued, "they don't let students go back into the stacks. They're afraid we might get the books mixed up or steal them or something. When you want a book, you turn in a request slip for it and they send a page boy after it."

"This is all very informative, Clothilde, but I wish you had picked another time to tell it to me. I've got a theme to write."

Clothilde's big blue eyes narrowed craftily into little blue eyes. "Some students, Dobie, are allowed to go back in the stacks. Some graduate students and a few seniors get permits. If they are doing the kind of work that requires a lot of books at hand, particularly obscure books, they can get stack permits. Then they can go back themselves and find the books they want without tying up the librarian and several page boys. These"—she waved the two white cards—"are stack permits."

"I still don't see——"

"I borrowed them," said Clothilde, "from a couple of graduate students I know. With these cards we can get into the stacks."

"But how is all this going to get my theme written?" We were almost at the library now.

"Dobie Gillis, you dope. I swear if you didn't have freckles and a crew haircut, I'd quit going with you in a minute. Don't you understand? We're going back in the stacks and find some old book of essays that nobody has ever heard of and you'll copy one of the essays and that will be your theme."

I stopped dead. "Clothilde," I whispered, "you can't mean it."

"Why not? It's foolproof. There won't be any record of you ever having seen the book. You won't turn in a request slip for it, so nobody will be able to check back through the slips. We're going into the stacks on somebody else's permit, so you can't be checked that way. You're not going to take the book out, so there won't be a withdrawal record on your library card. I've got pencil and paper in my purse. You'll copy the essay out of the book while you're in the stacks. Then you'll put the book back exactly where you found it. Then we'll leave and nobody will be the wiser."

I sat down beside a tree in front of the library and pulled her down beside me. "Clothilde," I said, "why don't we just get a couple of revolvers and go hold up a filling station?"

"This is no time to be finicky, Dobie. You know very well you'll never get that theme written."

"True," I said after a short silence.

"Then come on into the library. It's eight-thirty."

"I can't, Clothilde. My conscience would never stop bothering me."

She pulled me to my feet. She's quite a bit stronger than I am.

"Anyway," I protested, "it's not safe. How can we be sure that Mr. Hambrick, my English instructor, hasn't read the book that I'm going to copy the essay out of?"

Clothilde smiled. "I was hoping you'd ask that question. Come along. I'll show you."

She dragged me into the library, up the stairs and to the main desk. "Stop perspiring, Dobie," she whispered. "We don't want anybody to remember us." She showed the two stack permits to the librarian. The librarian nodded us back into the stacks.

The stacks filled me with awe. They consisted of metal bookshelves arranged in banks. Each bank was seven tiers high, and each tier was six feet tall. At the head of each bank was a metal spiral staircase, wide enough for only one person. Narrow catwalks ran along each tier, and the various banks were joined by other catwalks. The whole thing, I thought, looked like the cell blocks you see in prison movies. I shuddered at the significance of the comparison.

"Come along," said Clothilde. "The essay collections are in the seventh tier of the fourth bank. Hurry. We haven't much time."

We raced through the catwalks. Our footsteps echoed metallically, and I expected to hear sirens and see spotlights at any moment. I felt like James Cagney in "White Heat."

When we got to the essay shelves, Clothilde said, "Now,

quickly, look for a book with a lot of dust on it. Don't take any clean ones."

We looked for a few seconds, and I found a volume gray with dust. I pulled it off the shelf. "This all right, Clothilde?"

She took it. She opened the book and looked at the record card in the envelope pasted inside the cover— the card that the library files when you take out a book. "This one is no good," said Clothilde. "The card shows that this book was last taken out in 1942. It's not very likely, but there's just a chance that your English instructor was the one who took it out. If so, he might still remember the essays. We don't have to take chances; we can find a book that hasn't been taken out for at least ten years. Then, even if your instructor was the one who checked out the book, there's not much chance that he'll remember it."

"You thought any about becoming a gun moll?" I asked.

"Hurry, Dobie, it's a quarter to nine."

We found a couple more dusty volumes, but their cards showed that they had both been out of the library within the past ten years. At seven minutes to nine, we found the right one.

"This is perfect," said Clothilde, holding up the book, a slim collection called *Thoughts of My Tranquil Hours* by one Elmo Goodhue Pipgrass. Mr. Pipgrass's picture appeared on the frontispiece—a venerable gentleman with side whiskers and a white string tie. The record card in the book was almost lily white. The book had been taken out only once, and that was 'way back in 1926.

"This is perfect," Clothilde repeated. "The book has only been taken out once. It was published"—she looked at the title page—"in 1919. The picture of Pipgrass on the frontispiece shows that he was a man of at least seventy at that time. He's certainly dead now, so you don't even have to worry about plagiarism."

"Plagiarism!" I exclaimed. "You didn't say anything about that before."

"No use to alarm you, Dobie," she said. "Hurry up now. It's five minutes to nine. Here's pencil and paper."

"Plagiarism," I muttered.

"Hurry, Dobie. For Pete's sake, hurry."

With the greatest reluctance, I took pencil and paper and began to copy the first essay in *Thoughts of My Tranquil Hours.* It started like this:

Who has not sat in the arbor of his country seat, his limbs composed, a basin of cheery russet apples at his side, his meerschaum filled with good shag; and listened to the wholesome bucolic sounds around him: the twitter of chimney swifts, the sweet piping of children at their games, the hale cries of the countryman to his oxen, the comfortable cackling of chickens, the braying of honest asses; and felt his nostrils deliciously assailed with aromas from the kitchen: the nourishing saddles of beef, the beneficent gruels, the succulent tarts; and basked in the warmth of sun and earth, full bounty of abundant nature; and thought, "Of what moment is man's travail for gain, his mad impetus toward wealth, his great unsettled yearning for he knows not what, when all about him if he would but perceive are the treasures of the globe, more precious far than any jewel which lies deep beneath virgin earth across unplumbed and perilous seas?"

That was the first sentence, and the shortest one. I scribbled furiously until I had the whole thing down, and we left. We got out of the library at five seconds before nine.

Outside, I turned on Clothilde. "Why did I ever listen to you?" I cried. "Not only do I run the risk of getting kicked out of school in disgrace, but I've got to worry about getting arrested for plagiarism too. And to top it all off, the essay stinks. He'll probably flunk me on it anyway."

"Could you have done better?" she asked.

"That's not the point——"

"Come on," she said impatiently. "We'll miss the last show at the Bijou."

I didn't enjoy the show one bit. I enjoyed even less handing in my theme on Friday morning. As I laid the sheets on Mr. Hambrick's desk, visions of policemen and hanging judges and prison gates sped through my head. My forehead was a Niagara of perspiration.

"You feel all right, Mr. Gillis?" asked Mr. Hambrick.

"Yes, sir," I said. "I feel fine, thank you."

"I was just asking," he said. "I don't really care."

The gaiety of the week end failed to cheer me up. Dressed as a buccaneer on Saturday night, I swashbuckled listlessly through a masquerade party, and on Sunday I sat like a lump all through a hayride, never once joining in the four hundred verses of "Sweet Violets."

In my English class Monday morning I was resigned. I was prepared for the worst. I wasn't even surprised when Mr. Hambrick told me to stay behind at the end of the class.

"I want to talk to you about the theme you turned in Friday, Mr. Gillis," said Mr. Hambrick when we were alone in the room.

"Yes, sir," I said, my voice hitting high C above middle E.

"Frankly," he continued, "I was amazed at that theme. Until Friday, Mr. Gillis, I had merely thought of you as dull."

"Yes, sir."

"But now I know I was wrong. The trouble with you is that you're archaic."

"Huh?"

"You're archaic. You're way behind the times. You were born one century too late. And," he added, "so was I. I tell you, Mr. Gillis, I have no regard for modern writing. It all seems like gibberish to me—all that clipped prose, that break-neck pacing, that lean objectivity. I don't like it. I think writing should be leisurely and rich. Sentences should be long and graceful, filled with meaning and sensitive perception. Your theme, Mr. Gillis, is a perfect example of the kind of writing I most admire."

"Call me Dobie," I said genially.

"I'm going to give you an 'A' on that theme, and I hope in the future you will write some more like it."

"You bet," I said. "I know just where to get them."

"And if you're ever free on a Sunday afternoon, I'd be pleased if you'd stop at my place for a cup of tea. I'd like to talk to you about a novel I've been toying with. It's a great deal like your stuff."

"Sure, pal. Now if you'll give me my theme, I've got to get on to my next class."

"Ah," he smiled, his neutral-colored eyes twinkling behind tortoise-shelled glasses, "I'm afraid I can't do that. I've got a little surprise for you, Mr. Gillis. I've entered your theme in the Minnesota Colleges Essay Contest."

I just made it to a chair. "Again," I gasped. "Say that again."

"I've entered your theme in the Minnesota Colleges Essay Contest," he repeated. "It's a competition sponsored once a year by the State Board of Education for all the colleges in Minnesota—the university and Hamline and Macalester and St. John's and all the rest. The contest is judged by the four members of the Board of Education and the winner gets a free cruise on the Great Lakes."

"Please!" I screamed. "I don't want to be in any contest. I don't want to win a Great Lakes cruise. I get seasick. Even in a bathtub I get seasick."

"Come, come, Mr. Gillis. You mustn't be so modest. Let me give you a bit of advice, my boy. I was just like you are. I hid my light beneath a bushel too. Now look at me —teaching English to a bunch of little morons. No, Mr. Gillis, you've got to assert yourself, and I'm going to see that you do."

"Please, Mr. Hambrick," I begged tearfully.

"It's too late anyhow. As soon as I read your theme last Friday night, I put it in the mail immediately. It's already in the hands of the Board of Education. The results of the contest will be announced Thursday. Well, goodbye, Mr. Gillis. I must rush to my next class."

I sat there alone in that classroom for two hours.

Twitching. Just twitching. I couldn't even think. I just twitched. Like a horse dislodging flies. Then, skulking behind trees, I walked to my room, crawled into bed, and moaned until sundown.

In the evening I found Clothilde and, with a great deal of bitterness, told her the whole story.

"That's not good," said Clothilde. Sharp, that girl.

"I wish," I said honestly, "that I had never set eyes on you."

"Don't be vile, Dobie. Let's figure something out."

"Oh no you don't. I'm through listening to you. Tomorrow I'm going to Mr. Hambrick and confess everything. There's nothing else to be done, no matter what *you* say."

"Dobie, you really work hard at being stupid, don't you? That's the silliest thing I ever heard. Really, I don't see what you have to worry about. If Mr. Hambrick, a professional English instructor, didn't suspect anything, what makes you think that the members of the State Board of Education are going to get wise?"

"Now you listen to me, Clothilde. Every minute I delay my confession just makes it worse for me. It stands to reason that at least one of those Board of Education members has read Elmo Goodhue Pipgrass's *Thoughts of My Tranquil Hours.*"

"Fat chance," sneered Clothilde.

"No, Clothilde. I won't do it. I know I'm going to get caught, and I might just as well get it over with."

"Honestly, I've never met such a yuck. You'll never get caught, you poor goof. They'll read the theme and reject it, and the whole business will be over with. The things you find to worry about."

"Good God, girl. What if I win the contest?"

"With that corn?" she asked. "Ha. Honestly, Dobie."

Then she argued some more, but I was firm as a rock. It took her more than twenty minutes to talk me into it.

For the next three days, as tragedy mounted on tragedy, I was numb with fear. I'll tell you how numb I was: a practical joker in my political science class put a tack on my seat and I sat on it all through the class.

Tuesday Mr. Hambrick said to me, "Good news, Mr. Gillis. Your essay has advanced into the quarter-finals."

I nodded mutely and went out into the hall and twitched some more.

Wednesday Mr. Hambrick said to me, "Great news, Mr. Gillis. Your essay is now in the semi-finals."

I tried to confess everything to him then, but all that came out of my throat were hoarse croaks.

And Thursday the walls came tumbling down.

"Mr. Gillis," said Mr. Hambrick, "Something very curious has happened. Your essay won out in the semi-finals and was entered in the finals. Your competition in the finals was an essay by a young man named Walter Bradbury from Macalester College. Mr. Bradbury's essay is a description of iron mining in northern Minnesota. Now, it happens that of the four members of the Board of Education, two are from the Iron Range district. Those two insist on awarding the prize to Mr. Bradbury. But the other two members want to give you the prize. Neither side will yield."

"I'll withdraw," I said hastily.

"That's noble of you," said Mr. Hambrick, "but it won't be necessary. The Board of Education has agreed to call in an impartial judge to pick the winner. You and Mr. Bradbury are to go over to the Board of Education office in the state capital this afternoon for the final judging. I've arranged transportation for you."

"Mr. Hambrick," I pleaded desperately. "Let them give the prize to Bradbury. The sea air will do him good."

"Nonsense." Mr. Hambrick laughed. "You're sure to win. I know the judge they picked is going to favor you. He's a distinguished essayist himself, who used to write much as you do. He's been in retirement for many years at a cottage near Lake Minnetonka. He's very old. Possibly you may have heard of him. His name is Elmo Goodhue Pipgrass."

Click. I heard a distinct click in my head. Then a terrifying calm came over me. I felt drained of emotion, no

longer capable of fear or worry. I felt as a man must feel who is finally strapped into the electric chair.

"There will be a car in front of the Administration Building in thirty minutes to take you to the state capitol," said Mr. Hambrick.

"Yes, sir," I said. My voice seemed to be coming from far away.

"Good luck—Dobie."

I found Clothilde and told her everything—told it to her evenly, coolly, without rancor.

"I'm going to the state capitol with you," she said. "I'll think of something."

I patted her shoulder. "Thank you, Clothilde, but no. It will be better if we break clean—now. I don't want you to be known as the consort of a criminal. Your whole life is ahead of you, Clothilde. I don't want to be a burden to you. Try to forget me, Clothilde, if you can. Find somebody new."

"You're awfully sweet, Dobie."

"And so are you, Clothilde, in an oblique way."

"Then this—this is it?"

"Yes, Clothilde. This," I said, the little muscles in my jaw rippling, "is it."

"What are you going to do with those two tickets to Tommy Dorsey tonight?"

"They're yours, Clothilde." I handed them to her and added with a wry smile, "I won't be needing them."

We shook hands silently, and I went off to the Administration Building and got into the car and was driven to the state capitol.

I went into the Board of Education office and was directed to the conference room. This room contained a long mahogany table with five empty chairs behind it. There were two chairs in front of the table, and in one of them sat a young man wearing a sweater with "Macalester" emblazoned across the front.

"You must be Walter Bradbury." I said. "I'm Dobie Gillis."

"Hi," he said. "Sit down. They'll be here in a minute."

I sat down. We heard footsteps in the hall.

"Here they come," said Bradbury. "Good luck, Dobie."

"Oh no, no, no!" I cried. "Good luck to you. I want you to win. With all my heart I do. Nothing would make me happier."

"Why, thanks. That's awfully decent of you."

They came in, and the pit of my stomach was a roaring vastness. The four members of the Board of Education were dressed alike in dark business suits and looked alike—all plumpish, all bespectacled, all balding. With them, carrying a gnarled walking stick, was Elmo Goodhue Pipgrass, the littlest, oldest man I had ever seen. His side whiskers were white and wispy, the top of his head egg-bald. His eyes looked like a pair of bright shoe buttons. He wore a high collar with a black string tie, a vest with white piping, and congress gaiters. He was ninety-five if he was a day.

One of the Board members took Pipgrass's arm to assist him. "Take your big fat hand off my arm," roared Pipgrass. "Think I'm a baby? Chopped half a cord of wood this morning, which is more than you ever chopped in your whole life. Weaklings. The government is full of weaklings. No wonder the country's gone to rack and ruin. Where are the boys?"

"Right over here, Mr. Pipgrass," said a Board member, pointing at Bradbury and me. "See them?"

"Of course I see them. Think I'm blind? Impudence from public servants. What's the world come to? Howdy, boys." He nodded vigorously at a hall tree. "Sit down."

"They are sitting down, Mr. Pipgrass," said a Board member. "Over here."

"Whippersnapper," muttered Pipgrass. "I remember when they built this state capitol. Used to come and watch 'em every day. If I'd known they were going to fill it with whippersnappers, I'd have dynamited it."

"Mr. Pipgrass," said a member gently, "let's get to the essays. The boys have to get back to school."

"Essays? What you talking about? I haven't written an essay since 1919."

Suddenly hope was reborn within me. The man was senile. Maybe I'd get away with it. Maybe . . .

"The boys' essays, Mr. Pipgrass. You're to pick the best one, remember?"

"Certainly, I remember. Think I'm an idiot? Who's Bradbury?"

"I, sir," said Bradbury.

"Ah. You're the fool who wrote an essay on iron mining. Iron mining! Why didn't you write one on plumbing? Or garbage disposal?"

I felt a sinking sensation.

"Or roofing?" continued Pipgrass. "Or piano tuning? Iron mining! What kind of subject is that for an essay? And furthermore you split four infinitives. And don't you know that a compound sentence take a comma between clauses? Great Jehoshaphat, boy, where'd you ever get the idea you could write?"

Bradbury and I trembled, each for his own reason.

"Gillis," said Pipgrass. "Gillis, you pompous, mealy-mouthed little hack. Who told you that you were a writer?" He picked up my essay, held it a half inch before his face, and read, " 'Who has not sat in the arbor of his country seat . . .' " He threw down the essay. "I'll tell you who has not sat in the arbor of his country seat. You haven't. Bradbury hasn't. All of these four fat fellows haven't. Who the devil has got a country seat? What the devil *is* a country seat? Who talks about country seats these days? What kind of writer are you? Who said you were a writer? Can't anybody write in this confounded state?

"It's a sorry choice," said Pipgrass, "that I have to make between these two wights. Neither of 'em can write worth a nickel. But if I must choose, give the prize to Bradbury."

A great weight rolled off my back. A film dropped from my eyes. I smiled a real smile.

Now they were all around Bradbury shaking his hand, but none so heartily as I. I waited until they all left the room and then I got down on my knees and sent off six quick prayers. I mopped my forehead, my cheeks, my chin, my neck, and my palms, and then I went into the hall.

Pipgrass was waiting for me.

"You Gillis?" he asked.

I nodded, holding the doorjamb for support.

He took my arm. "I was tempted to give you the prize, boy. Mighty flattering to know that people are still reading *Thoughts of My Tranquil Hours* after all these years."

Then he was gone down the corridor, chuckling and running his walking stick across the radiators.

She Shall Have
Music

Ski-U-Mah was in a bad way.

"Something's got to be done," said Dewey Davenport, the editor. "There's no time to waste. School starts in two weeks."

"Let's hear from the circulation manager," said Boyd Phelps, the associate editor.

They looked at mè.

"Oh. Pansy, Pansy!" I cried.

Dewey put a sympathetic arm around my shoulder. "Get hold of yourself, Dobie," he said kindly. "Pansy is gone."

"Gone," I sighed. "Gone."

"And Ski-U-Mah," he continued, "is in trouble."

"You must forget Pansy," said Boyd. "Try to think about Ski-U-Mah."

"I'll try," I whispered bravely.

"That's my boy," said Dewey, giving me a manly squeeze. "Now, Dobie, you're the circulation manager. Have you got any ideas to build circulation?"

But I wasn't listening. Pansy's face was before me. The fragrance of her hair was in my nostrils, and I thought my heart would be rent asunder. Pansy, Pansy, lost and taken from me! "Pansy," I moaned.

"Dobie, she's not dead," said Dewey with a touch of annoyance. "Don't be so emotional."

"I'm an emotional type," I cried, and indeed I was. That had been the seat of my trouble with Pansy—my inability to contain my emotions in her presence. The very sight of her had made me spastic with delight. I had twitched, quivered, shaken, jumped, and whirled my arms in concentric circles. Pansy had looked kindly upon my seizures, but her father, a large, hostile man named Mr. Hammer, had taken an opposite view. He had regarded me with a mixture of loathing and panic, and finally, fearing for his daughter's safety, he had sent her away from me.

I had met Pansy the year before at the University of Minnesota where we had both been freshmen. I had been immediately smitten. And who would not have been? What healthy male would not have succumbed to her wise but frolicsome eyes, her firm but succulent lips, her sturdy but graceful throat, her youthful but mature form? What man could have resisted her manifold graces, her myriad charms? Certainly not I.

I plunged headlong into the pursuit of Pansy, and I am pleased to report that my suit met with success. After she overcame her initial alarm at my exuberance, her affection for me burgeoned until it matched mine for her. Then I made a mistake: I asked to meet her folks.

"Gee, I don't know, Dobie," she said doubtfully. "Maybe we'd better wait awhile. I'm not sure how you and Daddy will get along."

"If he's your father, I'll love him," I replied, nibbling her fingers ecstatically.

"Maybe so," she said, "but I'm worried about what he'll think of you. He's a gruff, sober type, and—no offense, Dobie—you're kind of nuts."

"Nonsense," I cried, leaping goatlike around her. "Take me to him."

"All right," she said with a conspicuous lack of enthusiasm. "But, Dobie, listen. Try to make your outbursts as minor as possible, will you? Nothing massive if you can help it."

"Don't worry about a thing," I assured her, and we went forthwith to her costly home in South Minneapolis.

I must say that I have never behaved quite so calmly as on my first meeting with Mr. and Mrs. Hammer. I did not leap or spin; I did not cavort, dance, kick, whistle, or roll. Perhaps I twitched a few times, and I blinked a bit, and once I wrapped my hands around my head, but otherwise I was the very model of sedateness.

I cannot say, however, that the Hammers were impressed with my composure. Mrs. Hammer showed only slight evidences of nervousness—just an occasional shudder—but Mr. Hammer was openly agitated. He kept casting me looks of wild surmise; several times he inquired pointedly about my health. When I finally made my goodbyes, he was flagrantly relieved.

"Well, what did they think of me?" I asked Pansy when I saw her on campus the next day.

"Mother seemed disinclined to discuss you," Pansy replied, "but Daddy was quite frank. He said you ought to be locked up."

"Hm," I said glumly, but my spirits instantly revived. "Don't worry, Pansy," I said confidently. "I will win him."

Overriding Pansy's earnest protests, I continued to call on her at home. The results were not what I had hoped. Her mother contrived to be absent whenever I came. Her father's attitude toward me progressed from dismay to consternation; his color evolved from a brackish white to a mottled purple. It seemed that there was nothing I could do to please him. My friendly grimaces only served to infuriate him. Whenever I gave him a jovial slap on the back, he recoiled in horror. It got so that the mere sight of me would set him whimpering. "No good will come of all this," I told myself darkly.

I was right. Mr. Hammer sent Pansy away from me. Instead of letting her return to the University of Minnesota for her second year, he shipped her off to New York City. There she was to live with her aunt Naomi, a flinty old spinster, and attend Barnard College. Aunt Naomi had been instructed by Mr. Hammer to reject all phone calls and destroy all letters coming from me.

And now here I was in the Ski-U-Mah office, separated from my true love by half a continent. If only I had some money, I would have flown to her, but I was as poor as a churchmouse and twice as miserable.

"Dobie," said Dewey Davenport sharply. "Will you pay attention? Ski-U-Mah may have to close this year. We've only got two weeks before school starts. We need circulation. That's your job, remember?"

"Pansy," I said, biting my lip. "Pansy."

"Ah, what's the use?" said Boyd Phelps dejectedly. "Even if Dobie had any ideas, it wouldn't help. Let's face it, Dewey. Ski-U-Mah is a dead duck. The day of the college humor magazine is over—not only at Minnesota, but everywhere. College kids have outgrown all that rah-rah stuff. The war, the A-bomb, the H-bomb—who's thinking about fun and jokes these days?"

"Nuts," replied Dewey. "College kids are still college kids. They're still smooching and driving convertibles and cutting classes and looking for laughs."

"Not like they used to," said Boyd.

"Yes," Dewey insisted. "Here, I'll give you an example. Remember last year when Benny Goodman played a dance at the gym? They had the biggest turnout in the history of the university. Does that sound like everyone is sitting around moping?"

Yes, I thought, a soft smile playing on my lips, yes, I remembered that dance. Pansy and I had gone together. Oh, how we danced, how we stomped, how we whirled, how we hopped, how we—CLANG! A bell sounded in my head with the noise of a thousand alarms. An idea had come to me, an overpoweringly perfect idea! Everything was solved. *Everything!*

"I've got it!" I cried, jumping up and down. "I've got it!"

Dewey and Boyd looked at me askance.

"That's our answer," I said eagerly. "That's how we'll get subscriptions for Ski-U-Mah. We'll hold a dance."

"I don't get it," confessed Dewey.

"Look," I said. "We'll hire a big-name band—Benny Goodman or Tommy Dorsey or somebody like that. Then instead of charging a dollar for a ticket to the dance as they usually do, we'll charge two dollars. The extra dollar will be for a year's subscription to Ski-U-Mah. It's a package deal, don't you see?"

Dewey and Boyd considered the idea. "Not bad, not bad," said Boyd.

"No, it isn't," Dewey agreed. "It's a fine idea. There's only one hitch. Have we got enough money in our treasury to hire a big-name band?"

"We've got exactly one thousand dollars," said Boyd.

Dewey shook his head. "Not enough."

"We could try," said Boyd. "Why don't we write a letter to the booking office in New York and see what they say?"

"No, no," I cried quickly. That wasn't what I had in mind at all. A trip to New York was the most important part of my plan—to see Pansy again, to live again, to be a whole man again. But, of course, I did not intend to mention *that* to Dewey and Boyd.

"Don't send a letter," I said. "They'll only turn you down. You can't expect them to send Goodman or Dorsey all the way to Minneapolis for a thousand dollars—unless, of course, some young clean-cut fellow appeared in person and persuaded them."

"You, for instance?" said Dewey.

"Not to brag," I said, lowering my eyes modestly, "but you will go far to find another as young and clean-cut as I."

"And you think they'd listen to you at the booking agency?" asked Dewey.

"I'm sure of it," I declared. "I'll come up there all neat and tweedy with my cowlick standing up and a lump in my throat and I'll tell them all about our great Ski-U-Mah tradition and how the magazine is in trouble and how everything depends on them, and then I'll look up at them, trusting-like, with my eyes shining and a crooked little smile on my face. How can they resist me?"

I took a stance and showed Dewey and Boyd what I meant.

"He *does* look kind of appealing," Boyd admitted.

"Yes, he does," said Dewey, examining me minutely.

I nodded energetically.

Dewey waved a forefinger under my nose. "Now listen, Dobie, your expenses have to come out of this thousand dollars, so don't waste a cent. You'll travel by bus and you'll sleep at the Y.M.C.A. Eat as little as possible. Do your business as soon as you get to New York and then come right back. Understand?"

"Yes, yes, yes," I said, clapping my hands rapidly. I was going to Pansy, to Pansy, to Pansy! Oh, happy day! Oh, kind fate!

The next morning Dewey and Boyd took me down to the Minneapolis bust depot and put me on a bus for New York. I got off the bus in St. Paul and transferred to an airplane. A tedious bus journey was not to be borne; I had to get to Pansy quickly. I felt a little guilty about spending the extra fare, but after all, twenty or thirty dollars would hardly make any difference when I came to hire a band.

As soon as I landed at LaGuardia Field, I rushed to the telephones. I looked up Aunt Naomi's number and dialed it with trembling fingers. An unfriendly feminine voice answered. "Hello?"

"Hello," I said. "Is Miss Pansy Hammer there?"

"Who is calling?" asked the voice suspiciously.

"This is Mr. Johnson. I am the dean of Barnard College."

"You sound awfully young to be a dean," said doubting old Aunt Naomi.

"Yes, don't I?" I replied with a hollow laugh. "In many quarters I am known as 'The Boy Dean.' . . . But enough of this chitchat. I'm a very busy dean. Please put Miss Hammer on."

There was a short pause and then I heard Pansy's voice. "Pansy!" I cried, vibrating joyously in the phone booth. "Pansy, it's Dobie Gillis. I've come to you, my darling. I'm here in New York."

I heard a sharp intake of breath and then she said in a carefully controlled tone, "Why yes, Dean. When do you want to see me?"

"Smart girl," I said approvingly. "Can you meet me in an hour at the airlines terminal building in New York?"

"I'll be there," she said. "Goodbye, Dean."

Rubbing my hands gleefully, I got into the airlines limousine and rode to New York. I was at the terminal building in thirty minutes. That left another thirty minutes to wait before Pansy would arrive. I was much too agitated to sit still so I decided to go out for a short walk. I skipped down Forty-second Street and turned up Fifth Avenue. The gaily decorated shopwindows matched my festive mood, and soon I was singing lustily. As I passed a florist's shop, my attention was seized by a display of orchids in the window. No ordinary orchids these, but blooms as white and soft and lovely as Pansy herself. I went into the store.

A clerk slithered toward me. "M'sieu?" he lisped.

"I would like a dozen of those orchids," I cried, "for the loveliest girl in the world."

"*Quel sentiment!*" he exclaimed, embracing me.

"Quickly," I said, disengaging myself. "She comes."

He swished into action and in a trice he had fashioned a corsage that made me limp with rapture. "That will be one hundred dollars," he said.

I turned ashen.

"A glass of water?" asked the clerk. "A light wine, perhaps?"

I shook my head, for already I was recovering. After all, what difference would a hundred dollars make when it came to hiring the band? The whole deal was to be based on my personal appeal anyhow. In fact, the less money I had, the more pathetic I would be. And besides, it would be worth a hundred dollars to see Pansy's face when I gave her the corsage—even if the hundred dollars was not mine. Smiling, I handed the clerk the money and raced back to the terminal building.

She was waiting for me. Fifty feet separated us when I first spied her. I covered the distance in three great bounds. "My darling, my angel, my dove!" I cried, kissing her with random accuracy.

"Dobie," she said simply.

We clung.

"A corsage," I said, handing her the orchids.

"Oh, they're lovely. . . . But it's kind of big for a corsage, isn't it, Dobie?"

"I'll fix that," I said and draped the orchids around her neck like a Derby winner.

We laughed. Then, suddenly serious, I clutched her again. "I've missed you so much, Pansy."

She nuzzled my jowl. "And I you," she confessed.

"Is there no chance that your father will let you come back to Minnesota?"

She shook her head. "No. I start classes at Barnard next week."

"Shall I survive this year?" I croaked hoarsely, smiting my forehead.

"I know," she said softly. "It's going to be awful." She wept, nor were my eyes dry.

"But away with this gloom!" I cried. "At least we will have a little time together. Let us be gay. Let us taste all the joys that this great city has to offer."

"Heigh-ho," she replied airily and linked her pretty round arm in mine.

Some may censure me for my activities on that evening, and I cannot really defend myself. Admittedly the expenditure of two hundred dollars of Ski-U-Mah funds was not an honorable act. I can only say this: I did not know when I would see Pansy again; there was money in my pocket; the town was full of pleasures; and even under the best of circumstances, I cannot think clearly in Pansy's presence. Call me wayward if you will; that was the way things were.

We had cocktails at the Plaza. We had dinner at 21. We saw *South Pacific*. We had supper at the Stork. We danced at El Morocco. We drove four times around Central Park in a hansom. After I took Pansy home, I checked into the Waldorf. No lesser hostelry would suit my exalted mood.

In the morning, of course, things were different. I lay between the Waldorf's excellent sheets jack-knifed with panic. It took a long time before I was able to get up and count my money. Then, having discovered that my funds totaled slightly over six hundred dollars, I oozed to the floor in a moaning mound. An hour was spent in this position. At length I rallied myself. There was nothing to do but go down to the booking agency and try to get a band for six hundred dollars.

I prepared myself carefully. I yanked my cowlick until it stood like a mast on my scalp. I buffed my face until it shone like a Baldwin apple. I practiced digging my toe into the rug. I stood before the mirror and ran through my repertory of winsome expressions. Then I went down to the booking agency.

The booking agency occupied one large, shabby office. Part of the office was a waiting room; the other part, separated by a waist-high railing, was the business office. Seated on a bench in the waiting room were six huge, villainous-looking women. At a desk behind the railing sat a cadaverous, blue-jowled man with eyes like two bits of anthracite. The six women were staring dully at the floor as I entered. They looked at me with momentary interest, then sighed and returned their gaze to the floor. I approached the man behind the railing.

"How do you do?" I said with a fetching smile. "I'm Dobie Gillis from the University of Minnesota Ski-U-Mah."

He gave me a quick appraisal with his anthracite eyes and said nothing.

"I'd like to book a band for a dance at the university on September 14. I had in mind someone like Benny Goodman or Tommy Dorsey."

"How much loot you got?" asked the man.

"I beg your pardon?"

"Money. How much?"

"First," I said, smiling warmly, "I'd like to tell you a little about Ski-U-Mah. It's one of the finest traditions at the University of Minnesota. Yes, indeed. We all have a soft spot in our hearts for Ski-U-Mah out there. We certainly do."

"How much loot?"

"Ski-U-Mah, you'll be distressed to hear, has fallen on evil days. But now, with your co-operation, we believe we can save it. I know, of course, that sentiment and business are not supposed to mix, but I always say, scratch a businessman and you'll find a heart of pure gold."

"Kid, come on already. How much loot?"

"Six hundred dollars," I said, turning a look upon him that would melt a stone.

"Goodbye, kid," he said.

"Vaughan Monroe would do," I said, tugging my cowlick.

"Kid," he said, "you got rocks in your head?"

"Perhaps," I said in a cracking treble, "you could suggest somebody?"

"Nobody," he said flatly, "will go to Minneapolis for six hundred dollars."

"Ahem, ahem." The sound came from behind me. I turned and saw the largest of the six women on the bench rise and approach me with a gigantic grin.

"Kid," said the man at the desk, "you're in luck. This is Happy Stella Kowalski and her Schottische Five. They just happen to be between bookings right now."

"Pleased to make your acquaintance, hey," said Happy Stella, crushing my hand in hers. The Schottische Five stood up and grinned fatly.

"You are a band?" I asked nervously.

"The best," roared Happy Stella. "Ask Al."

"The best," confirmed the man at the desk. "They play more Lithuanian weddings than any band on the entire Atlantic Seaboard."

"We're a riot, hey," confessed Stella, prodding me with her outsized forefinger. "We wear funny hats. We black our teeth. We play washboards, gaspipes, pots and pans, all kinds of funny stuff. We fracture the people."

"You mustn't take this unkindly, Happy Stella," I said, "but I've never heard of you."

"Kid, where you been?" asked Al. "This is the hottest combination in New York. You don't know how lucky you are to catch 'em between bookings."

I scratched my head uncertainly. "And they'll come for six hundred dollars?"

"Ordinarily, no," said Al. "For Ski-U-Mah, yes."

He whipped out a contract, gave me a pen, and guided my hand over the dotted line. Then I shook hands with Al and Happy Stella and the Schottische Five, Rutka, Sletka, Dombra, Simka, and Majeska—and left the office with a breast full of misgivings.

I had not done well; there was no gainsaying it. For a moment I toyed with the idea of not going back to Minneapolis, but finally dismissed the thought as cowardly. Besides, I didn't have enough money left to stay in New York. I went to the bus station, bought a ticket home with my remaining resources, and invested my last dime in a good-bye phone call to Pansy.

Aunt Naomi answered. "Hello," I said, "this is Mr. Johnson, the Boy Dean. I want to talk to Miss Hammer."

"I have called Barnard College," said Aunt Naomi icily. "There is no Mr. Johnson on the faculty. You are Dobie Gillis, and if you try to communicate with Pansy again I will call the police."

"Please, Aunt Naomi," I could hear Pansy saying, "just let me say goodbye to him."

"Very well," said Aunt Naomi. "But this is the last time, you understand?"

Pansy came on the phone. "How are you, Dobie dear?"

"Fine," I lied. There was no use to afflict her with my misery.

"Did you get Benny Goodman for your dance?"

"No," I said with a wan smile, "I got somebody better. Happy Stella Kowalski and her Schottische Five."

"Who?"

"It's a sensational new all-girl band. They fracture the people."

"That's nice, dear. When are you leaving?"

"In a few minutes."

"Oh, how I wish I were going back with you! I'll miss you so much, Dobie, so very much."

"Me too."

She sobbed briefly.

"Don't cry, dear," I soothed. "Maybe we'll be together soon."

"It can't be soon enough. When do you think you'll get back to New York?"

"Not," I said, "in the forseeable future."

"Oh, Dobie!" she wailed.

"Goodbye, Pansy, dear heart. I love you."

Gently I hung up the telephone and walked into the bus for Minneapolis.

Dewey and Boyd were waiting for me at the Minneapolis station. At first I tried to bluff it out. "Great news, fellows!" I shouted. "I booked Happy Stella Kowalski and her Schottische Five. What a coup for Ski-U-Mah!"

"Who?" said Dewey and Boyd with double horror.

I could not go on with it. Suddenly the truth came pouring from my lips, the whole horrible story. "But I'll pay back the money I spent," I said in conclusion. "I'll pay it back somehow."

"I know you will, Dobie," said Dewey wearily, without anger. "That's not the point. What happens to Ski-U-Mah now? How do we get anybody to buy tickets for Happy Stella Kowalski?"

"They'll close the magazine this year if we don't make a profit," said Boyd.

"I know," I replied miserably. "I'm just a no-good rat."

Dewey put his arm around my slumping shoulders. "All right, Dobie. What's done is done. Now the only thing left is to try to sell some dance tickets."

And try we did. We collared everybody on campus; we applied all possible pressures. Our efforts were greeted with curt refusals, sometimes with astonishment. "Happy Stella who?" people would ask. When the night of the dance came around, we had sold exactly 150 tickets to an enrollment of 20,000 students.

At 7:30 on the night of the dance I was in the gymnasium disconsolately hanging bunting. Dewey was sitting on the bandstand with his chin in his hand. Boyd had gone down to the railroad station to pick up Happy Stella Kowalski and her Schottische Five, who were due to arrive at eight o'clock. Suddenly a large, purple-faced man came running wildly into the gymnasium—Mr. Hammer, Pansy's father.

He spied me on top of the ladder. "You!" he roared and shook me down like a ripe plum. "What have you done with her?"

"Hello, Mr. Hammer. Nice to see you. Done with whom?"

"You know very well who. Where's Pansy? Her aunt told me you saw her in New York. Now where is she?"

"Isn't she in New York?"

"Gillis, I'll strangle you," he yelled, lunging at me.

Dewey thrust himself hastily between us. "What's wrong, Mr. Hammer?" he asked.

"Pansy disappeared from her aunt's apartment in New York two days ago. Gillis engineered the whole thing. He's got her hidden someplace. I'm calling the police. I'm charging him with abduction." All this delivered in a deafening bellow.

Dewey turned to me. "Dobie, tell the truth. Do you know anything about this?"

"So help me, Dewey," I cried earnestly, "not a thing."

"You're lying, you kidnaper," screamed Mr. Hammer. "I'm calling the police. Where is she?"

"Mr. Hammer, be reasonable," said Dewey. "Dobie's been here for more than a week. How could he have kidnaped Pansy?"

"He's got accomplices. He's a fiend. I knew he should

have been locked up the minute I laid eyes on him. I'm calling the police."

At this point Boyd came walking in with Stella Kowalski and her Schottische Five. They were dressed in motley dirndls about the size of pyramidal tents. On their heads they wore hideous hats with ratty plumes. Under their arms they carried washboards, pipes, pots, plungers, and assorted hardware. Their front teeth were blacked out.

We stood and stared at them, even Mr. Hammer. Then suddenly I saw that the Schottische Five were six, and the sixth one was not a huge, gross cow moose of a woman. She was slender and fair and beautiful even with blacked-out teeth. She was Pansy!

"Pansy!" The cry escaped my lips.

"Aha!" roared Mr. Hammer. "Caught you red-handed." There was a telephone on the wall nearby. He seized it. "Police!" he shouted into the mouthpiece. "Send the patrol wagon. Send the riot squad. Send everything you've got!"

Happy Stella strode over and grabbed Mr. Hammer by the lapels. "What's with you?" she said dangerously.

"You'll find out when you're behind bars," replied Mr. Hammer, trying vainly to loose himself.

"Oh, you must be the old man," said Happy Stella. "Shame on you." She shook him until his eyes rolled freely in their sockets.

"Assault and battery," mumbled Mr. Hammer. "Kidnaping plus assault and battery. That's what I'm charging you with."

Pansy stepped forward. "There was no kidnaping," she said firmly. "I went to Happy Stella and asked her to take me with her. I thought Aunt Naomi might catch me if I tried running away alone."

"Don't say anything, Pansy," warned Mr. Hammer. "They've probably got you drugged."

"I am not drugged," said Pansy, stamping her foot. "I have never thought so clearly in my life."

She walked over and took my arm. "Daddy," she said

with as much dignity as a girl can muster who has blacked-out teeth, "I love Dobie and I'm going to stay with him. If you send me to New York again, I'll run away again. I don't care where you send me, I'm not going to be kept apart from Dobie."

"Whatsa matter with you, hey?" demanded Happy Stella, giving Mr. Hammer another shake. "Can't you see these kids wanna be together? So what if Dobie is a little screwy? Who ain't?"

Mr. Hammer opened and closed his mouth several times, carp-fashion. "All right," he snarled at last. "All right. But, Pansy, you keep that maniac out of my house, do you hear? And if, God forbid, you should ever marry him, I don't want to hear about it."

Suddenly the street outside the gym was filled with the scream of sirens. The police Mr. Hammer had called were arriving. Car after car pulled up in front of the gym with a horrific screeching of tires. Dozens of cops with drawn guns came pouring into the gym. And behind the police came a mob of students, pressing in to see what the excitement was.

Dewey leaped up as though he had been stung. "Dobie, Boyd!" he yelled with wild excitement. "Get to the door. Don't let any students in unless they buy tickets. Here's how we save Ski-U-Mah."

We rushed forward and threw ourselves across the door. "Two dollars!" shouted Dewey to the mob. "Two dollars to come inside. Hurry, hurry, hurry!"

The students in the front ranks started to dig in their pockets for money, but the mob behind them surged forward. It looked for a moment as though Dewey, Boyd, and I would be swept aside. But Happy Stella came running to our aid with her Schottische Five. Buttressed by the musical Amazons, we were able to hold fast until the crowd got their money out. Then we stood aside and let them rush through, throwing currency at us as they passed. The money showered over us, piled up on the floor around us.

It is difficult to describe what was happening inside

the gym. I was not on the sinking *Titanic* or at the Battle
of Gettysburg, but these, I think, are fair comparisons.
All I can remember is humanity flooding in, filling the
gym to the walls, and cops yelling and brandishing guns,
and Mr. Hammer trying vainly to make explanations over
the din, and Dewey cackling hysterically as he counted
money.

It took about an hour before the cops left, casting foul
looks at Mr. Hammer as they went. Then Dewey got up
and made an announcement to the assemblage, telling
them that they were at a dance. There was a little sullen
muttering, but most of them took the news calmly. Then
Happy Stella and her Schottische Five started to mount
the bandstand.

"Miss Hammer," I said with a courtly bow to my true
love, "may I have the honor of the first dance?"

"The second dance," she said. "I'm playing a wash-
board solo for the first dance."

She gave me a loving, black-toothed smile and joined
the musicians.

Love Is a Fallacy

Cool was I and logical. Keen, calculating, perspicacious, acute and astute—I was all of these. My brain was as powerful as a dynamo, as precise as a chemist's scales, as penetrating as a scalpel. And—think of it!—I was only eighteen.

It is not often that one so young has such a giant intellect. Take, for example, Petey Bellows, my roommate at the university. Same age, same background, but dumb as an ox. A nice enough fellow, you understand, but nothing upstairs. Emotional type. Unstable. Impressionable. Worst of all, a faddist. Fads, I submit, are the very negation of reason. To be swept up in every new craze that comes along, to surrender yourself to idiocy just because everybody else is doing it—this, to me, is the acme of mindlessness. Not, however, to Petey.

One afternoon I found Petey lying on his bed with an expression of such distress on his face that I immediately diagnosed appendicitis. "Don't move," I said. "Don't take a laxative. I'll get a doctor."

"Raccoon," he mumbled thickly.

"Raccoon?" I said, pausing in my flight.

"I want a raccoon coat," he wailed.

I perceived that his trouble was not physical, but mental. "Why do you want a raccoon coat?"

"I should have known it," he cried, pounding his temples. "I should have known they'd come back when the Charleston came back. Like a fool I spent all my money for textbooks, and now I can't get a raccoon coat."

"Can you mean," I said incredulously, "that people are actually wearing raccoon coats again?"

"All the Big Men on Campus are wearing them. Where've you been?"

"In the library," I said, naming a place not frequented by Big Men on Campus.

He leaped from the bed and paced the room. "I've got to have a raccoon coat," he said passionately. "I've got to!"

"Petey, why? Look at it rationally. Raccoon coats are unsanitary. They shed. They smell bad. They weigh too much. They're unsightly. They——"

"You don't understand," he interrupted impatiently. "It's the thing to do. Don't you want to be in the swim?"

"No," I said truthfully.

"Well, I do," he declared. "I'd give anything for a raccoon coat. Anything!"

My brain, that precision instrument, slipped into high gear. "Anything?" I asked, looking at him narrowly.

"Anything," he affirmed in ringing tones.

I stroked my chin thoughtfully. It so happened that I knew where to get my hands on a raccoon coat. My father had had one in his undergraduate days; it lay now in a trunk in the attic back home. It also happened that Petey had something I wanted. He didn't *have* it exactly, but at least he had first right on it. I refer to his girl, Polly Espy.

I had long coveted Polly Espy. Let me emphasize that my desire for this young woman was not emotional in nature. She was, to be sure, a girl who excited the emotions, but I was not one to let my heart rule my head. I wanted Polly for a shrewdly calculated, entirely cerebral reason.

I was a freshman in law school. In a few years I would
be out in practice. I was well aware of the importance of
the right kind of wife in furthering a lawyer's career. The
successful lawyers I had observed were, almost without
exception, married to beautiful, gracious, intelligent
women. With one omission, Polly fitted these specifica-
tions perfectly.

Beautiful she was. She was not yet of pin-up propor-
tions, but I felt sure that time would supply the lack. She
already had the makings.

Gracious she was. By gracious I mean full of graces.
She had an erectness of carriage, an ease of bearing, a
poise that clearly indicated the best of breeding. At table
her manners were exquisite. I had seen her at the Kozy
Kampus Korner eating the specialty of the house—a sand-
wich that contained scraps of pot roast, gravy, chopped
nuts, and a dipper of sauerkraut—without even getting
her fingers moist.

Intelligent she was not. In fact, she veered in the opposite direction. But I believed that under my guidance
she would smarten up. At any rate, it was worth a try.
It is, after all, easier to make a beautiful dumb girl smart
than to make an ugly smart girl beautiful.

"Petey," I said, "are you in love with Polly Espy?"

"I think she's a keen kid," he replied, "but I don't know
if you'd call it love. Why?"

"Do you," I asked, "have any kind of formal arrangement with her? I mean are you going steady or anything
like that?"

"No. We see each other quite a bit, but we both have
other dates. Why?"

"Is there," I asked, "any other man for whom she has
a particular fondness?"

"Not that I know of. Why?"

I nodded with satisfaction. "In other words, if you were
out of the picture, the field would be open. Is that right?"

"I guess so. What are you getting at?"

"Nothing, nothing," I said innocently, and took my
suitcase out of the closet.

"Where you going?" asked Petey.

"Home for the week end." I threw a few things into the bag.

"Listen," he said, clutching my arm eagerly, "while you're home, you couldn't get some money from your old man, could you, and lend it to me so I can buy a raccoon coat?"

"I may do better than that," I said with a mysterious wink and closed my bag and left.

"Look," I said to Petey when I got back Monday morning. I threw open the suitcase and revealed the huge, hairy, gamy object that my father had worn in his Stutz Bearcat in 1925.

"Holy Toledo!" said Petey reverently. He plunged his hands into the raccoon coat and then his face. "Holy Toledo!" he repeated fifteen or twenty times.

"Would you like it?" I asked.

"Oh yes!" he cried, clutching the greasy pelt to him. Then a canny look came into his eyes. "What do you want for it?"

"Your girl," I said, mincing no words.

"Polly?" he said in a horrified whisper. "You want Polly?"

"That's right."

He flung the coat from him. "Never," he said stoutly.

I shrugged. "Okay. If you don't want to be in the swim, I guess it's your business."

I sat down in a chair and pretended to read a book, but out of the corner of my eye I kept watching Petey. He was a torn man. First he looked at the coat with the expression of a waif at a bakery window. Then he turned away and set his jaw resolutely. Then he looked back at the coat, with even more longing in his face. Then he turned away, but with not so much resolution this time. Back and forth his head swiveled, desire waxing, resolution waning. Finally he didn't turn away at all; he just stood and stared with mad lust at the coat.

"It isn't as though I was in love with Polly," he said thickly. "Or going steady or anything like that."

"That's right," I murmured.

"What's Polly to me, or me to Polly?"

"Not a thing," said I.

"It's just been a casual kick—just a few laughs, that's all."

"Try on the coat," said I.

He complied. The coat bunched high over his ears and dropped all the way down to his shoe tops. He looked like a mound of dead raccoons. "Fits fine," he said happily.

I rose from my chair. "Is it a deal?" I asked, extending my hand.

He swallowed. "It's a deal," he said and shook my hand.

I had my first date with Polly the following evening. This was in the nature of a survey; I wanted to find out just how much work I had to do to get her mind up to the standard I required. I took her first to dinner. "Gee, that was a delish dinner," she said as we left the restaurant. Then I took her to a movie. "Gee, that was a marvy movie," she said as we left the theater. And then I took her home. "Gee, I had a sensaysh time," she said as she bade me good night.

I went back to my room with a heavy heart. I had gravely underestimated the size of my task. This girl's lack of information was terrifying. Nor would it be enough merely to supply her with information. First she had to be taught to *think*. This loomed as a project of no small dimensions, and at first I was tempted to give her back to Petey. But then I got to thinking about her abundant physical charms and about the way she entered a room and the way she handled a knife and fork, and I decided to make an effort.

I went about it, as in all things, systematically. I gave her a course in logic. It happened that I, as a law student, was taking a course in logic myself, so I had all the facts at my finger tips. "Polly," I said to her when I picked her up on our next date, "tonight we are going over to the Knoll and talk."

"Oo, terrif," she replied. One thing I will say for this girl: you would go far to find another so agreeable.

We went to the Knoll, the campus trysting place, and we sat down under an old oak, and she looked at me expectantly. "What are we going to talk about?" she asked.

"Logic."

She thought this over for a minute and decided she liked it. "Magnif," she said.

"Logic," I said, clearing my throat, "is the science of thinking. Before we can think correctly, we must first learn to recognize the common fallacies of logic. These we will take up tonight."

"Wow-dow!" she cried, clapping her hands delightedly.

I winced, but went bravely on. "First let us examine the fallacy called Dicto Simpliciter."

"By all means," she urged, batting her lashes eagerly.

"Dicto Simpliciter means an argument based on an unqualified generalization. For example: Exercise is good. Therefore everybody should exercise."

"I agree," said Polly earnestly. "I mean exercise is wonderful. I mean it builds the body and everything."

"Polly," I said gently, "the argument is a fallacy. *Exercise is good* is an unqualified generalization. For instance, if you have heart disease, exercise is bad, not good. Many people are ordered by their doctors not to exercise. You must *qualify* the generalization. You must say exercise is *usually* good, or exercise is good *for most people*. Otherwise you have committed a Dicto Simpliciter. Do you see?"

"No," she confessed. "But this is marvy. Do more! Do more!"

"It will be better if you stop tugging at my sleeve," I told her, and when she desisted, I continued. "Next we take up a fallacy called Hasty Generalization. Listen carefully: You can't speak French. I can't speak French. Petey Bellows can't speak French. I must therefore conclude that nobody at the University of Minnesota can speak French."

"Really?" said Polly, amazed. "*Nobody?*"

I hid my exasperation. "Polly, it's a fallacy. The generalization is reached too hastily. There are too few instances to support such a conclusion."

"Know any more fallacies?" she asked breathlessly. "This is more fun than dancing even."

I fought off a wave of despair. I was getting nowhere with this girl, absolutely nowhere. Still, I am nothing if not persistent. I continued. "Next comes Post Hoc. Listen to this: Let's not take Bill on our picnic. Every time we take him out with us, it rains."

"I know somebody just like that," she exclaimed. "A girl back home—Eula Becker, her name is. It never fails. Every single time we take her on a picnic——"

"Polly," I said sharply, "it's a fallacy. Eula Becker doesn't cause the rain. She has no connection with the rain. You are guilty of Post Hoc if you blame Eula Becker."

"I'll never do it again," she promised contritely. "Are you mad at me?"

I sighed. "No, Polly, I'm not mad."

"Then tell me some more fallacies."

"All right. Let's try Contradictory Premises."

"Yes, let's," she chirped, blinking her eyes happily.

I frowned, but plunged ahead. "Here's an example of Contradictory Premises: If God can do anything, can He make a stone so heavy that He won't be able to lift it?"

"Of course," she replied promptly.

"But if He can do anything, He can lift the stone," I pointed out.

"Yeah," she said thoughtfully. "Well, then I guess He can't make the stone."

"But He can do anything," I reminded her.

She scratched her pretty, empty head. "I'm all confused," she admitted.

"Of course you are. Because when the premises of an argument contradict each other, there can be no argument. If there is an irresistible force, there can be no immovable object. If there is an immovable object, there can be no irresistible force. Get it?"

"Tell me some more of this keen stuff," she said eagerly.

I consulted my watch. "I think we'd better call it a night. I'll take you home now, and you go over all the things you've learned. We'll have another session tomorrow night."

I deposited her at the girls' dormitory, where she assured me that she had had a perfectly terrif evening, and I went glumly home to my room. Petey lay snoring in his bed, the raccoon coat huddled like a great hairy beast at his feet. For a moment I considered waking him and telling him that he could have his girl back. It seemed clear that my project was doomed to failure. The girl simply had a logic-proof head.

But then I reconsidered. I had wasted one evening; I might as well waste another. Who knew? Maybe somewhere in the extinct crater of her mind a few embers still smoldered. Maybe somehow I could fan them into flame. Admittedly it was not a prospect fraught with hope, but I decided to give it one more try.

Seated under the oak the next evening I said, "Our first fallacy tonight is called Ad Misericordiam."

She quivered with delight.

"Listen closely," I said. "A man applies for a job. When the boss asks him what his qualifications are, he replies that he has a wife and six children at home, the wife is a helpless cripple, the children have nothing to eat, no clothes to wear, no shoes on their feet, there are no beds in the house, no coal in the cellar, and winter is coming."

A tear rolled down each of Polly's pink cheeks. "Oh, this is awful, awful," she sobbed.

"Yes, it's awful," I agreed, "but it's no argument. The man never answered the boss's question about his qualifications. Instead he appealed to the boss's sympathy. He committed the fallacy of Ad Misericordiam. Do you understand?"

"Have you got a handkerchief?" she blubbered.

I handed her a handkerchief and tried to keep from screaming while she wiped her eyes. "Next," I said in a carefully controlled tone, "we will discuss False Analogy. Here is an example: Students should be allowed to look at their textbooks during examinations. After all, surgeons have X rays to guide them during an operation, lawyers have briefs to guide them during a trial, carpenters have blueprints to guide them when they are building a house. Why, then, shouldn't students be allowed to look at their textbooks during an examination?"

"There now," she said enthusiastically, "is the most marvy idea I've heard in years."

"Polly," I said testily, "the argument is all wrong. Doctors, lawyers, and carpenters aren't taking a test to see how much they have learned, but students are. The situations are altogether different, and you can't make an analogy between them."

"I still think it's a good idea," said Polly.

"Nuts," I muttered. Doggedly I pressed on. "Next we'll try Hypothesis Contrary to Fact."

"Sounds yummy," was Polly's reaction.

"Listen: If Madame Curie had not happened to leave a photographic plate in a drawer with a chunk of pitchblende, the world today would not know about radium."

"True, true," said Polly, nodding her head. "Did you see the movie? Oh, it just knocked me out. That Walter Pidgeon is so dreamy. I mean he fractures me."

"If you can forget Mr. Pidgeon for a moment," I said coldly, "I would like to point out that the statement is a fallacy. Maybe Madame Curie would have discovered radium at some later date. Maybe somebody else would have discovered it. Maybe any number of things would have happened. You can't start with a hypothesis that is not true and then draw any supportable conclusions from it."

"They ought to put Walter Pidgeon in more pictures," said Polly. "I hardly ever see him any more."

One more chance, I decided. But just one more. There is a limit to what flesh and blood can bear. "The next fallacy is called Poisoning the Well."

"How cute!" she gurgled.

"Two men are having a debate. The first one gets up and says, 'My opponent is a notorious liar. You can't believe a word that he is going to say.' . . . Now, Polly, think. Think hard. What's wrong?"

I watched her closely as she knit her creamy brow in concentration. Suddenly a glimmer of intelligence—the first I had seen—came into her eyes. "It's not fair," she said with indignation. "It's not a bit fair. What chance has the second man got if the first man calls him a liar before he even begins talking?"

"Right!" I cried exultantly. "One hundred per cent right. It's not fair. The first man has *poisoned the well* before anybody could drink from it. He has hamstrung his opponent before he could even start. . . . Polly, I'm proud of you."

"Pshaw," she murmured, blushing with pleasure.

"You see, my dear, these things aren't so hard. All you have to do is concentrate. Think—examine—evaluate. Come now, let's review everything we have learned."

"Fire away," she said with an airy wave of her hand.

Heartened by the knowledge that Polly was not altogether a cretin, I began a long, patient review of all I had told her. Over and over and over again I cited instances, pointed out flaws, kept hammering away without letup. It was like digging a tunnel. At first everything was work, sweat, and darkness. I had no idea when I would reach the light, or even *if* I would. But I persisted. I pounded and clawed and scraped, and finally I was rewarded. I saw a chink of light. And then the chink got bigger and the sun came pouring in and all was bright.

Five grueling nights this took, but it was worth it. I had made a logician out of Polly; I had taught her to think. My job was done. She was worthy of me at last. She was a fit wife for me, a proper hostess for my many mansions, a suitable mother for my well-heeled children.

It must not be thought that I was without love for this girl. Quite the contrary. Just as Pygmalion loved the perfect woman he had fashioned, so I loved mine. I decided to acquaint her with my feelings at our very next meeting. The time had come to change our relationship from academic to romantic.

"Polly," I said when next we sat beneath our oak, "tonight we will not discuss fallacies."

"Aw, gee," she said, disappointed.

"My dear," I said, favoring her with a smile, "we have now spent five evenings together. We have gotten along splendidly. It is clear that we are well matched."

"Hasty Generalization," she repeated. "How can you say that we are well matched on the basis of only five dates?"

I chuckled with amusement. The dear child had learned her lessons well. "My dear," I said, patting her hand in a tolerant manner, "five dates is plenty. After all, you don't have to eat a whole cake to know that it's good."

"False Analogy," said Polly promptly. "I'm not a cake. I'm a girl."

I chuckled with somewhat less amusement. The dear child had learned her lessons perhaps too well. I decided to change tactics. Obviously the best approach was a simple, strong, direct declaration of love. I paused for a moment while my massive brain chose the proper words. Then I began:

"Polly, I love you. You are the whole world to me, and the moon and the stars and the constellations of outer space. Please, my darling, say that you will go steady with me, for if you will not, life will be meaningless. I will languish. I will refuse my meals. I will wander the face of the earth, a shambling, hollow-eyed hulk."

There, I thought, folding my arms, that ought to do it.

"Ad Misericordiam," said Polly.

I ground my teeth. I was not Pygmalion; I was Frankenstein, and my monster had me by the throat. Frantically I fought back the tide of panic surging through me. At all costs I had to keep cool.

"Well, Polly," I said, forcing a smile, "you certainly have learned your fallacies."

"You're darn right," she said with a vigorous nod.

"And who taught them to you, Polly?"

"You did."

"That's right. So you do owe me something, don't you, my dear? If I hadn't come along you never would have learned about fallacies."

"Hypothesis Contrary to Fact," she said instantly.

I dashed perspiration from my brow. "Polly," I croaked, "you mustn't take all these things so literally. I mean this is just classroom stuff. You know that the things you learn in school don't have anything to do with life."

"Dicto Simpliciter," she said, wagging her finger at me playfully.

That did it. I leaped to my feet, bellowing like a bull. "Will you or will you not go steady with me?"

"I will not," she replied.

"Why not?" I demanded.

"Because this afternoon I promised Petey Bellows that I would go steady with him."

I reeled back, overcome with the infamy of it. After he promised, after he made a deal, after he shook my hand! "The rat!" I shrieked, kicking up great chunks of turf. "You can't go with him, Polly. He's a liar. He's a cheat. He's a rat."

"Poisoning the Well," said Polly, "and stop shouting. I think shouting must be a fallacy too."

With an immense effort of will, I modulated my voice. "All right," I said. "You're a logician. Let's look at this thing logically. How could you choose Petey Bellows over me? Look at me—a brilliant student, a tremendous intellectual, a man with an assured future. Look at Petey —a knothead, a jitterbug, a guy who'll never know where his next meal is coming from. Can you give me one logical reason why you should go steady with Petey Bellows?"

"I certainly can," declared Polly. "He's got a raccoon coat."

The Sugar
Bowl

My pretty girl was like a melody, but she wouldn't play for a nickel. In fact, I believe she was only dimly aware that nickels were being minted. Coins of such lowly denomination were outside her ken; folding money, on the other hand, she understood intimately. Everything she liked ran into staggering figures. If I took her to a movie, it could not be at a soberly priced neighborhood house; it had to be at a plushy downtown theater, and moreover, we had to sit in the loges. For her aftertheater snack she scorned the lowly hamburger; nothing less than a lobster salad would do. Nor would she ride in a streetcar; it had to be a taxi. Nor eat at a drugstore; it had to be a café with a headwaiter named Pierre. Nor dance to a jukebox; it had to be a live orchestra of no fewer than sixteen pieces.

Her tastes were nothing short of ruinous to me. I was a member of the most underprivileged class in the world—the freshman class. I received from my cruel father an allowance that, if carefully husbanded, would provide me with three tiny meals a day and a quarter for Saturday nights. A girl like Thalia Menninger (for that was her

53

name) was wildly beyond my means. Why then, you may ask, did I cling to her?

If you could but see her, you would not need to ask. One look at her expensive hair, her costly eyes, her exorbitant skin, her overpriced torso, her bankrupting legs, and you would understand. You would cry, even as I, "Hang the expense! I got to have this dame!"

So I borrowed. I borrowed from Paul. Then I borrowed from Peter, but not to pay Paul. Paul remained unpaid, as did Sam and Bill and Ed and everybody else I could persuade to lend me money. By the middle of the semester my credit rating was so low that it would have brought a blush to the cheeks of Dun and Bradstreet themselves.

One day—I had a date with Thalia that evening—I went around to everybody I knew to try to borrow a few dollars. They all said no. They also said other things, too painful to repeat here, but the gist was that my credit was as exhausted as credit can get. So when I went to pick up Thalia at the girls' dormitory that night, I was entirely without funds.

No, that is not quite accurate. I did have one dollar. It was not, however, a spending dollar. It was a silver dollar with a bullet hole in the center, given to me by my grandfather on his deathbed. He had made me promise to keep it always. This dollar, he had told me, had saved his life during the Spanish-American War. This had seemed odd to me, since Grandpa had spent the Spanish-American War as a recruiting sergeant in Omaha, but one does not argue with an old gentleman in his last hours, so I had made the required pledge. Now, having given my word, I naturally could not break it.

I sat nervously in the lounge of the girls' dormitory, waiting for Thalia to come downstairs and nursing a pale hope that she would consent to devote this evening to a long walk. The hope went a-glimmering as soon as she appeared. She was wearing the least probable walking costume I have ever seen. Her dress was a froth of diaphanous ruffles; her shoes were little rhinestoned dainties with soles as thin as onion-skin and heels four inches high.

"Hi, Dobie," she chirped. "Let's go dancing. I feel so desperately much like dancing tonight. Don't you?"

"No," I said truthfully.

"Come on, Dobie. We've got to get in training for the prom."

"The prom?" I said fearfully.

"The Freshman Prom. Don't tell me you didn't know about it. It's a week from tonight. Oh, what a desperately wonderful affair it's going to be—Harry James and a grand march and everybody goes formal. Isn't that desperate?"

I ran my finger around the inside of my collar. "Do you happen to know," I whispered hoarsely, "how much tickets cost?"

"Only ten dollars a couple."

A moan escaped my lips.

She looked at me sharply. "What's the matter, Dobie?"

"Nothing. Nothing at all."

"We *are* going to the prom, aren't we?"

"Sure, Thalia, sure—that is, if it's possible."

"What do you mean—if it's possible? Listen, Dobie, I don't intend to miss a desperately wonderful affair like the prom."

"We'll go," I assured her. "Don't worry." Somehow, somewhere, I would borrow the money.

"Good," said Thalia. "Now where will we dance tonight? The Trocadero? The Idle Hour? The Persian Palms?"

"How about going for a walk instead?" I said, blinking my eyes hopefully.

"A walk?" she gasped, as though I had suggested robbing a poor box.

"Good exercise," I said casually. "Builds the wind. Believe me, Thalia, in the troubled times we live in, there's nothing quite so important as a good wind."

"Dobie, don't be so desperately ridiculous. Come on now. Let's go dancing."

"The fact is," I mumbled, digging my toe into the rug, "I'm a little short of money right now. It's only temporary, of course."

Her eyes widened with outrage. "How could you ask me on a date when you didn't have any money?" she demanded.

"Aw, Thalia, don't be mad. I thought you might like to go for a nice long walk."

"What do you think I am—a mailman?" she retorted hotly.

"Aw, Thalia——"

"How long are you going to be broke?"

"Not long. Not long at all."

"Are you going to be able to buy tickets for the Freshman Prom?" she asked, fixing me with a piercing glare.

"Sure, sure," I said with what I hoped would be a reassuring chuckle, but it turned out to be a hysterical giggle.

"Listen, Dobie, I've had other offers. Please say so if you can't raise the money."

A bolt of fear stabbed into my heart. "Thalia," I cried in anguish, "you wouldn't go with anybody but me, would you? I thought we had an understanding."

"My understanding," she said coldly, "was that you were going to take me out and show me a good time. That does not include long walks. Now when are you going to buy the tickets for the prom?"

"Tomorrow," I promised in desperation.

"Very well. Meet me in the library at three o'clock. If you don't have the tickets then, I'm going to accept another date. Now go." She pointed a peremptory forefinger at the door.

I shambled out of the dormitory, cursing her for a heartless golddigger and myself for an idiot. Why didn't I give her up? All right, so she was beautiful. So she had hair like fine-spun gold. So she had eyes that were fire and ice, lips that were a succulent red challenge, clavicles that arched classically, a flawlessly bifurcated bosom, a waist that first tapered and then billowed with precisely the proper abundance, legs that age could not wither nor custom stale.

I sighed. My question was answered. That is why I did not give her up: the hair, the eyes, the lips, the clavicles, and all the other above-mentioned members. Reason enough, you would agree if you knew Thalia.

As I walked miserably away from the dormitory, a girl came running up behind me and grabbed my arm. An unnerving sight she was. Her black hair stood out like a bramblebush. Her untidy dress seemed to be fashioned of a material closely resembling burlap. On her feet she wore ragged objects made of rope and canvas. "Yes?" I said uneasily.

"My name is Fannie Jordan," she said. "You excite me."

This intelligence failed to fill me with delight. "That's nice," I mumbled and tried to wrest my arm from her grasp.

Her pressure increased. "I was in the lounge while you were arguing with Thalia. Obviously she is the wrong girl for you. I am the right girl. Let's go steady."

I looked at her askance. "Isn't this rather sudden?"

She shrugged. "Why go through the stupid ritual of courtship? Are we people or whooping cranes?"

In her case there was some room for doubt, but I did not comment. "Please, Miss Jordan," I said. "I've got an appointment."

"We would make ideal mates," she said, and a shiver ran up my spine. "We are both young, both well formed, both intelligent. Why shilly-shally? Give me a kiss."

I broke into a dead run. She, however, clung to my arm and kept pace with me. "Note," she cried, "the condition I'm in. I can run like a deer. I can swim like a fish. I can lift my own weight. I can operate a drill press. I have all my teeth."

I stopped. Clearly I could not outrun her. "Miss Jordan," I panted, "be good enough to release me."

She tugged on my arm. "Where," she demanded, "can you find another girl with musculature and brains like mine? I'm not only strong; I'm also an intellectual. I happen to be a regular member of Professor Wycliffe's open house."

"I'm glad for you," I said. "Now if you'll let me go——"

"You don't seem impressed," she said. "Don't you know about Professor Wycliffe's open house?"

"No," I admitted. "You must tell me about it sometime —some *other* time." I tried to jerk away.

"Professor Wycliffe," she went on, holding fast, "used to teach modern literature here at the university. He's been retired now for several years, but he still conducts an informal discussion group at his home—only for exceptionally gifted students, of course. It's an open house that goes on every day—sandwiches, cakes, cookies, and wonderful discussions of modern literature. Go steady with ma, and I'll make you a member of the group."

"No, thanks," I declined with a shudder.

"You'll love Professor Wycliffe," she insisted. "Very fine man, very learned, very generous. Of course, he's got a lot of money, but he's not stingy with it like some rich people. Do you know that he keeps a sugar bowl filled with money on the mantel all the time?"

As the conversation took a fiscal turn, my interest increased. "Why," I asked, "does he keep a sugar bowl filled with money on the mantel all the time?"

"For members of the group who need to make a loan. The professor knows that students are always running short of money, so he's put this sugar bowl on the mantel. Whenever you want to borrow some money, you just take it out of the bowl. When you're ready to repay it, you just put it back in the bowl. You never have to say anything to anybody."

I felt life and hope returning to me. Here, if I was not mistaken, here in my darkest hour I had found my salvation.

"Let me get this straight," I said to Fannie. "Do you mean that you can actually borrow all the money you want and put it back whenever you like and you don't have to say a word to anybody?"

"That's right," she answered. "But that's not the attraction. It's the wonderful discussions that go on—so cogent, so penetrating, so vital to students of modern literature. You are, of course, a student of modern literature?"

"You bet," I lied stoutly. I don't know beans about modern literature. My field is mechanical engineering. To tell the truth, I don't know much about that either.

"I knew it," said Fannie. "I could tell by your smooth white forehead and your keen blue eyes. Give me a kiss."

"Later," I said, wrenching free with a colossal effort. "Let's go to Professor Wycliffe's house now."

"We can't. He doesn't allow students after seven o'clock. He reads in the evenings. . . . Come, embrace me."

I leaped behind an oak. "When can we go?" I asked.

"I'll meet you there at noon tomorrow. It's on Elm Street—the white house with the green shutters—— Dobie, come back here!"

"See you tomorrow," I cried, jumping on the back of a passing truck.

I was not easy in my mind as noon approached the next day. The thought of getting involved with Fannie Jordan filled me with consternation. Posing as a student of modern literature filled me with some more consternation. Still, how else could a deadbeat like me get hold of ten dollars? It had to be done.

Fannie was waiting for me on the porch of Professor Wycliffe's house. "Hello, dollface," she said, and lunged at me.

I held her off with judo. "Let's go inside," I urged. "I don't want to miss a minute of it."

I pulled her through the door and into a large Victorian living room. For a moment I was taken aback by the scene which greeted me there. This was my first close look at the campus literary set, and in appearance they were not reassuring. Some were frail and screechy. Some were gross and hairy, with dirty shirts and fingernails. Some were lean and intense, with eyes like live coals. But most unsettling of all were the women. Compared to the others, Fannie was a Powers model. Misshapen hulks they were, clad in pavement-colored frocks, their hair like untrimmed hedges, their voices strident as alarm bells, in each of their mouths a dangling cigarette.

There were perhaps thirty students in the room when we entered. They were seated in a ragged circle on the floor, arguing with deafening passion. At frequent intervals a tray of sandwiches or cookies would appear. There would be a half-minute's silence while the food was devoured and then, refreshed, they would resume their argument with increased volume.

In the center of the circle on a well-worn leather armchair sat Professor Wycliffe. Picture Santa Claus without the beard and you get the professor. He was the very personification of benevolence. His cheeks were rosy, his nose was rosier, his blue eyes twinkled with humor, his hair was snowy, his mouth wore a perpetual smile, his belly was benignly round.

Fannie brought me over to the professor and introduced me. "This is Dobie Gillis. He knows all about modern literature."

"I hope you don't mind my dropping in like this."

"Not at all. I'm always happy to have students of modern literature around me. Come over any time—before seven, that is. I read in the evenings."

"Thank you," I said.

"As you can hear," said the professor, pointing at the students with his pipe, "we are discussing existentialism. I'm sure you must have some opinions on the subject, Mr. Gillis."

"Indeed I do," I replied with diabolical cleverness. "But I am a terribly shy fellow. It will probably take weeks before I gather up enough nerve to join the discussion—maybe months."

"I understand," he said, nodding sympathetically. "You just sit down and listen and make yourself at home."

Fannie and I wedged our way into the circle. I assumed a listening attitude. I intended to stay in this position for

a half hour or so, just to make things look right, and then I would head for the sugar bowl. It stood, as advertised, on the mantel. Peeking over the top of it was the lovely green of U.S. currency. I had a sudden impulse to leap up and lunge at the bowl, but I held myself sternly in check. This operation had to be conducted slowly and with finesse; a premature move could louse up everything. So I contained myself and sat and listened.

What I heard might have been the conversation of Martians. "Sartre is a deviant," cried one of the students. "Subjective idealism can be interpreted on four levels," cried another. "Joyce's conception of archetypes derives from Kant's *Ding an Sich*," cried a third. "Kafka negated the image-myth," cried a fourth. "Rilke's *Zeitgeist* was post-oedipal," cried a fifth.

All of these unlikely statements were delivered with full throat and bristling conviction. Professor Wycliffe nodded benignly through the bedlam, puffing on his pipe, and occasionally tossing out an observation upon which the assemblage fell like a pack of hounds on a scrap of meat.

After a while I noticed that the student sitting on my left was taking no part in the conversation. He was a fat, pimply-faced fellow with a slack underlip, who sat and snored lightly until a plate of sandwiches appeared. Then as if by magic he would come awake. He would snatch up sandwiches with both hands, cram them into his mouth, and reach for more before the others could empty the plate. After eating he would shift position slightly and go right back to sleep until the next serving.

It came to me suddenly that I was not the only impostor in this room. Fat-Boy was another. It was clear that he didn't know modern literature from a hole in the ground. He was just a freeloader who came to stuff himself. I shrugged tolerantly; it was all right with me. I was hardly in a position to judge others.

Then an alarming thought crossed my mind. Was Fat-Boy only after a free meal? Or did he have his eye on the sugar bowl too? I rose to my feet. I couldn't take a chance.

Now, while Fat-Boy was asleep, I would have to make my move.

With elaborate casualness I crossed the room to the fireplace. I turned my back to the fireplace and placed my elbow on the mantel, my fingers not too close to the sugar bowl. I stood quite still for several minutes and pretended to listen to the discussion. Then, slowly, quarter inch by quarter inch, I moved my fingers toward the bowl. At last I made contact. Keeping my eyes front, I crooked my fingers over the edge of the bowl, dipped in, felt the coolness of the money.

Then I saw the professor looking at me. There was no friendliness in his glance now. There was speculation, even a little suspicion. Had he, I wondered, divined my scheme? Did he know that I was there under false pretenses, that my only interest was to latch onto the money in the sugar bowl? I withdrew my fingers hastily. I had obviously moved too fast. First I had to convince the professor that I was a student of modern literature; then I could go for the money. I would have to wait until tomorrow. I would have to risk losing the money to Fat-Boy. And also, I realized with a wrench of panic, I would somehow have to stall Thalia. That, I knew would not be easy, but it was the only course open to me. The sugar bowl was my last resort; I could not let my haste put that in jeopardy.

Casting the professor a disarming smile, I moved away from the mantel and resumed my place between Fannie and Fat-Boy. There I sat for two hours—nodding, frowning, cocking my head, rubbing my chin, winking, biting my lip, raising my eyebrows, making all sorts of intelligent grimaces to convince the professor that I understood the argument raging around me. Not until I was sure he was satisfied did I take my leave. "See you tomorrow," I called and, with a nervous look at Fat-Boy, I left the house.

Fannie caught up with me as soon as I reached the sidewalk. "Where are you going?" she demanded.

I turned and faced her squarely. Now that I had access

to Professor Wycliffe's house, I had no intention of keeping up any pretenses with this beast. "I am going to keep a date with my girl Thalia Menninger," I told her in loud, distinct tones.

"What's the matter with you?" she raged. "How can you possibly spend your time with a jitterbug like that?"

I bridled. "Thalia happens to be a very fine girl."

"Bah," replied Fannie Jordan. "She's not a girl at all. She's a confection."

"Miss Jordan, if you don't stop molesting me, I will call a policeman."

She seized both my shoulders in a grip of iron. "Tell me the truth. Is that what you want in a girl—chi-chi, frou-frou, fancy clothes, permanent waves?"

"Yes," I said. "Now please unhand me. I've got enough trouble."

"Are you blind, man?" she yelled. "Can't you see that I'm twelve times the woman she is? Look at me! I'm honest. I'm intelligent. I'm durable. I'm earthy. I'm built for a lifetime's service. Look at this pelvis. Go on, look!"

"Some other time," I said faintly. "I don't feel strong enough now. Won't you let me go?"

"Frou-frou and chi-chi—that's all you care about. Fool!" She thrust me from her with such force that I was sent reeling for a half block down the street. She went back into the professor's house, and I made my way to the library.

"Good news!" I cried as soon as I saw Thalia. "We're going to the Freshman Prom."

She extended her hand. "Show me the tickets."

"I'll have them tomorrow," I promised. "Absolutely. Without fail. For sure. Beyond a doubt. Most assuredly. Positively." And so on in this vein until Thalia was finally persuaded. She gave me until three o'clock the next afternoon to buy the tickets.

Promptly at noon the following day I entered Professor Wycliffe's salon. The same group littered the floor, making at least as much noise as previously. Fannie Jordan cast hot eyes on me as soon as I walked in. Giving her a wide berth, I moved over and took a place beside the dozing Fat-Boy. I let a half hour go by, during which I feigned interest in the gibberish, and then I walked boldly over to the sugar bowl and stuck my hand in. It was empty.

I gnashed my teeth. So Fat-Boy had beaten me to it after all. It could only have been Fat-Boy. Only a swine like that would have cleaned out the whole bowl. Anybody else would have left a little. It was my own fault, I thought bitterly. I should have taken a chance yesterday and grabbed the money. I should never have trusted Fat-Boy to keep his gluttonous hands off it. But the damage was done now. Sighing miserably, I slumped down on the floor.

One slim hope remained. I was sure that many of the students in the room were in debt to the sugar bowl. Perhaps some of them were going to repay their loans in the next few hours. Admittedly it was a slender possibility, but still it *could* happen. And if it did, I thought grimly, I would not lose out to Fat-Boy this time. I would snatch the money out of the bowl before he could even get his great hams off the floor.

I sat and waited until five minutes to three. Nobody came near the sugar bowl. There was nothing to do but pick up my aching bones and go face Thalia. With the gait of a convict walking down death row to the electric chair, I left Professor Wycliffe's house.

I arrived at the library with a plan. It was a desperate plan, born of desperation. The chances of its working were sickeningly minute. It was too complicated. It depended on too many factors. It contained too many stages, and each stage contained obstacles that were all but insurmountable. Yet it was the only plan that my beaten brain could produce. There was nothing to do but try it.

"Thalia, I haven't got the tickets," I said immediately upon meeting her. "I'll have them tonight. Will you wait until nine o'clock?"

"No," she said unequivocally.

I thereupon went into a plea that would have made William Jennings Bryan seem a mute and Demosthenes a high school valedictorian. Strangers had gathered around me and were weeping openly before I finished. Finally even Thalia was moved. She agreed to wait until nine o'clock. "But not one minute longer," she cautioned.

"I'll be at the girls' dormitory with the tickets at nine," I said, wiping my streaming brow. The first stage of my plan had ended successfully.

But in spite of my initial triumph, I had little confidence that the second stage would work. This stage involved getting Professor Wycliffe out of his house for several hours. Toward this end I had devised a really wild scheme. I phoned Professor Wycliffe. "Hello," I said. "This is Ernest Hemingway."

I heard a sharp intake of breath. "How do you do, Mr. Hemingway?" said the professor shakily.

"Tell you why I called, Wycliffe," I said briskly. "Happen to be going through Minneapolis. On my way to South Dakota for the pheasant shooting. Heard a lot about you. Best damn scholar of modern literature in the country. Been wanting to meet you for some time. How about dinner tonight?"

"I'd be honored, sir."

"Good man. Get down to Charlie's restaurant as soon as you can. I may be late, but wait for me."

"I'll leave right away."

"Good man. Good-by."

I hung up the telephone, scarcely believing my luck. Stage Two had worked. Still I took a dim view of the success of my plan. Stage Three lay ahead, and that was fraught with trouble. So was Stage Four. And Stage Five.

I waited outside the professor's house until I saw him leave. Then I went inside to put Stage Three in operation. This entailed getting the sugar bowl refilled.

The students were seated on the floor, still yocking away. Fannie glared at me balefully. Fat-Boy was dozing. I went to the professor's chair in the centre of the circle. I stood on the chair. "Attention!" I called.

They fell quiet and looked up at me.

"I have a very distressing announcement to make," I said. "I know how you all love the professor and appreciate all he has done for you. Well, here is your chance to do something for him. I have just learned that the professor is broke—absolutely penniless."

"But that's impossible!" cried a student. "He's got a great big trust fund."

"The trust fund is empty," I said sadly. "I heard about it today from an unimpeachable source. That's why we've got to help the professor. I know we can't do much, but at least we can all pay back the money we've taken out of the sugar bowl. How about it, kids? Let's put the money back."

"I still can't believe it," someone said. "How can he keep up this salon if he hasn't got any money?"

"It just happened today," I said. "That's why the professor had to go downtown."

"He didn't tell us anything about it," protested a student.

"Too proud," I said feverishly. Stage Three was misfiring badly. Nobody was making a move toward the sugar bowl. If only somebody would start, then I knew the rest would follow. "Who'll be the first to help out the dear professor?" I said with my most fetching smile.

Silence.

I felt vertigo setting in. Unless somebody would start this mob to the sugar bowl, I was a dead pigeon. I couldn't do it myself; I didn't have a penny.

Then I remembered the silver dollar with the bullet hole in the center. I had promised Grandpa that I'd never spend it, to be sure, but this wasn't really spending it. I would just be using it temporarily. I'd get it back when I raided the bowl later.

"I'll start," I announced in a loud tone.

I took the silver dollar out of my pocket and dropped it into the bowl. For an awful moment nobody moved to follow. Then they started to get up. One by one they passed the sugar bowl and dropped in their money. Even

Fat-Boy dropped in a couple of dollars—not nearly so much as he had taken out, that rat, but I was far too pleased to bear a grudge. Stage Three was a smashing success; the bowl was loaded with money.

"Thank you, thank you all," I cried happily.

As soon as they resumed their seats on the floor and returned to their debate, I embarked on Stage Four, which was to get Fat-Boy out of the way. I sat down beside him and nudged him awake. He looked at me with bleary, incurious eyes.

"Do you like plum pudding?" I said.

A flicker of interest danced across his face. He nodded his big head.

"I've got a plum pudding up in my room," I whispered to him. "It's been there since last Christmas. Plum pudding gets better the longer it stands, did you know that?"

His head went up and down again.

"My plum pudding is juicy and rich and yummy."

He smacked his slack lips.

"Would you like to have some?"

His head nodded until his ears flapped.

"Come with me," I said.

I took him up to my room. "It's in the closet," I said. "Go get it."

He went into the closet. I slammed the door behind him and turned the key. This time, by George, he wouldn't get to the sugar bowl before I did!

Now I was ready for Stage Five, which was to borrow ten dollars out of the bowl. I would wait until seven o'clock. By then, as I knew, the students would have left; the professor devoted his evenings to reading. Only this evening he was devoting to waiting for Ernest Hemingway. The house would be empty. All I would have to do was dash in, grab ten dollars—eleven, including my grandfather's dollar—and dash out again. Then I would buy two tickets to the Freshman Prom, show them to Thalia, and everything would be well again. My plan, crazy as it was, had worked!

Yet a couple of misgivings were in my mind as I ap-

proached the professor's house at seven-fifteen. What if
he had grown tired of waiting for Hemingway and come
home? What if there were still some students in the
room? Warily I tiptoed up to the front door. Inch by
inch I opened it. I peered inside. Nobody was there. Not
a sound could be heard. I heaved a great sigh of relief.
I crossed the living room, walked up to the mantel, stuck
my hand in the bowl. And it was empty.

What did I do then? I can't remember clearly. I think
I grasped my lapels and ripped them off. I think I banged
my head against the wall. I can't, as I say, remember. All
I know is that when I got home the lapels were off my
coat and there were lumps on top of my head.

I let Fat-Boy out of the closet. "That was a shoddy
trick," he complained and hit me in the eye, but I scarcely noticed it, so sunk in despond was I. He left and I flung
myself on my cot, my face to the wall. There I lay in
a black stupor. Nine o'clock came and went, but I did
not phone Thalia. She was lost, lost forever now. There
was no use trying any more.

About ten o'clock I heard a voice calling my name
outside my window. I groaned. The voice was Fannie
Jordan's. "Go away," I said in a lackluster tone. "Go
away."

"Come on out," she called.

"Go away," I repeated.

"Come on out or I'll throw rocks at your window."

Having no doubt that she would, I dragged my deplet-
ed frame out of the house.

"What do you want?" I said with dull anguish.

Then I saw her. My eyes bulged in my head. Was this
possible? Was the frump I knew the same girl who stood
before me now? For the transformation was unbelievable.
Her mop of black hair had been tamed into a chic feather
bob. Her bushy eyebrows were graceful arches. Her lips
were painted full and rosy. Her dress was of artfully cut
gossamer. Her slippers were suitable for drinking cham-
pagne out of.

"Are you satisfied now?" she said roughly. "This is the way you wanted it."

"Fannie, you're beautiful!" I exclaimed. "You're gorgeous! You're breathtaking!"

"Really, Dobie? Do you mean it?" There was no roughness in her tone now.

"You're the most beautiful creature I have ever seen!" Her blush was apparent even in the moonlight. "Don't kid me, Dobie," she said with lowered eyelids.

"I was never so serious in my life. Come on. I'll buy you a malted." Then I remembered. "Oops. I guess I won't buy you a malted. I'm broke."

"I've got some money," she said eagerly. "Come on."

So we went to the soda shoppe and drank our malteds, and I told her how beautiful she was until she fairly squirmed with pleasure. Then she paid for the malteds with a silver dollar that had a bullet hole in the center.

"Where," I said, white-faced, "did you get this dollar?"

"Out of the sugar bowl," she confessed in a small voice. "I know you'll think I'm horrid—I mean with the professor being broke and all that—but I had to borrow that money. Otherwise I wouldn't have been able to get a permanent and buy all these clothes. It was the only way I knew to get you, Dobie."

She looked at me timidly, seeking approval, and my heart was filled with love for her. "It's all right," I said, patting her newly manicured hand. "It's all right."

"I'll pay it back, Dobie," she assured me. "I'll save up my allowance and pay it back."

"I'm sure you will," I murmured, and then a new question came to mind. "Did you empty the sugar bowl yesterday too?"

She nodded. "Yes, but it wasn't enough. Without the money I took this afternoon, I wouldn't have been able to do all these things and get you. . . . I have got you, haven't I, Dobie?"

"Yes, dear Fannie, you've got me," I replied truthfully. "And now, how about a nice long walk?"

"Love it," said Fannie and linked her freshly massaged arm in mine.

Now I am going steady with Fannie Jordan. But am I better off than before? Curse it, no.

For a while things were fine. We took long walks and enjoyed simple pleasures, and I was able to clear up all my debts. But it could not last. Fannie, being a belle, finally got to thinking like a belle. Now nothing will do except downtown movies and swank cafés and live orchestras and taxis, and I am once more a deadbeat.

How can you win?

Everybody Loves
My Baby

It was Wednesday night, press time for the Koochiching County Weekly *Argus*. I sat checking the galley proofs while the governor read to me from the typewritten copy. (I call my father the governor. Actually, he isn't the governor at all. He did run for the Minnesota State House of Representatives once but was defeated by Quintus Schermerhorn, the incumbent.)

"Ready for the social notes, Dobie?" asked the governor. I nodded and he proceeded to read: " 'Wilhelm (Sonny) Rosencranz, son of Mr. and Mrs. Robert J. (Bob) Rosencranz, left Sunday for Hamline University. Good luck, Wilhelm (Sonny). . . . Emmaline (Emmy) Porter, daughter of Mr. and Mrs. Leroy (Fats) Porter, left Sunday for the St. Cloud State Teachers College. Best wishes, Emmaline (Emmy). . . . Norbert (Froggy) Holmquist, son of Mr. and Mrs. Olaf (Bet-a-Nickel) Holmquist, left Sunday for Gustavus Adolphus College. Knock 'em dead, Norbert (Froggy).' "

"I want to go to college too," I said.

"What for?" asked the governor.

He had me there.

"No, son," said the governor kindly, "you stay here

with me. I'll be retiring in twenty or thirty years, and the *Argus* will be all yours." He patted me on the shoulder and resumed reading the social notes. " 'Mr. and Mrs. Sven (Smiley) Bukema entertained Mrs. Bukema's maternal cousin, Miss Hulda Storch of Little Falls, over the week end. A good time was had by all. . . . Mr. Lynwood (Shorty) Mason won first prize in the Koochiching County Arts and Crafts Show with his statuette of Harold Stassen made entirely of bottle caps. Congratulations, Lynwood (Shorty). . . . Miss Daphne (Goat) Meltzer ——' "

A thought occurred to me. "Would you say that running a country weekly is complicated, the governor?" I asked.

The governor pulled a forelock thoughtfully as he had once seen William Allen White do in a newsreel. "Yes, son, I would," he replied after some deliberation.

"As complicated as law or medicine, for instance?"

"Yes," he said judiciously. "I believe it is."

"You wouldn't allow a man to practice law or medicine without a college degree, would you?"

"No."

"But you expect me to take over the *Argus* someday without ever having gone to college."

"Now, see here, Dobie——"

"Look at it this way, the governor," I said, pressing my advantage hard. "It would be an investment for you. Right now I'm not much help—just selling ads, setting type, reading proofs, and covering births, deaths, sports, and the county courthouse. But if I went to college and took a degree in journalism, I'd be equipped to be of some real help around here."

"You got a point, son," admitted the governor, and the next issue of the *Argus* carried an item that Dobie Gillis, son of Mr. and Mrs. Arthur W. (Ye Ed) Gillis, left Thursday for the University of Minnesota. Good luck, Dobie.

Now I have a little confession to make. Preparing myself to take over the *Argus* was only part of the reason I wanted to go to college; the rest of the reason was romantic. To be blunt, I was getting nowhere with the girls back home. The trouble was that I am a smallish, weakish fellow, and in my town the feminine taste runs to athletic types. All the plums were falling to the baseball and hockey teams. All I could get was what nobody else wanted, including me. Since I was a warm-blooded man of eighteen summers, the situation was not tolerable.

In college I knew it would be different. There things were on an intellectual plane. A man with a keen, incisive mind (like mine, for example) needed not to go loveless simply because he was not bulging with sinew. At the university, where an I.Q. counted more than a bicep, I was confident that I would find my mate.

Once at college I proceeded slowly. There was plenty to choose from; the campus was swarming with coeds—beautiful, well favored, and obviously intelligent, or else why would they be at college? Each day I went among them, peering into their faces, listening to their conversations, making notes, watching, waiting until the right one should appear.

One afternoon as I was walking across the campus with my head turned to observe a likely looking girl about ten yards to my left, I ran into the outstretched arm of the statue of William Watts Folwell, first president of the university. I fell to the turf, my head ringing like a great gong. Almost instantly a girl appeared beside me. She fell to her knees, cradled my reverberating head in her lap, stroked my brow, crooned compassionate endearments. I accepted her ministrations happily for several minutes and then opened my eyes. As soon as I could focus, I knew I had found the right one.

I don't want to say anything extravagant. I want to stick scrupulousy to the facts. I cannot state with any authority that this girl was the most beautiful girl in the world. Somewhere there may have been a girl with hair as blond and lips as red and ears as shell-like and skin as white and form as shapely as this girl's. I don't know; it's possible. But this I do know: nobody—living, dead,

or unborn—ever had or will have eyes like this girl had. They were blue, deep blue. They were large and wide, and in them was intelligence, sympathy, patience, humor, tolerance, tenderness, honesty, unselfishness, and a great overweening love for mankind.

"My name is Dobie Gillis," I said.

"You poor, poor boy," she replied. "You poor boy."

"Dobie Gillis," I repeated. "That's my name."

"Does it hurt terribly? Shall I call a doctor?"

"No, no. It's fine. Gillis. Dobie Gillis."

"I'm Sally Bean— No, don't get up. You lie there. I'll go get a cold compress."

"Don't go away," I cried, grasping her hand. "Just sit by me. That's a good girl."

"Is there anything I can do?"

"As a matter of fact, there is."

"Oh, good! What is it you want—a morphine Syrette, a traction splint, a transfusion, perhaps? Tell me."

"I want you to have dinner with me tonight."

"Of course, poor boy. Of course."

I beamed.

"I'm going out to dinner with a few boys. You come along."

I un-beamed. "A few boys?"

"Yes. Four or five."

"Sally," I said uncertainly, "why?"

"Why what?"

"Why four or five?"

"Because they asked me," she replied reasonably.

I tried to rise. She pushed me gently back. "Lie still, poor boy," she said.

"Sally, there's something I'd like to know."

"Of course, poor boy."

"Did these four or five fellows ask you to dinner all at once?"

"No, I believe Davy Ball asked me first. Then Joe Bracken, then Bob Sindorf, then Georgie Packer, and then Ellis Ford. Or maybe Ellis asked me before Georgie. I forget."

I rubbed my chin for a minute. "Sally, I don't mean to pry, but after Davy Ball asked you to dinner, why didn't you refuse all the other dates?"

"Because they would have been disappointed," said Sally.

There were two explanations: either the clout on the head had affected my hearing, or my leg was being pulled. "Sally," I said, "would you walk ten paces away and read me a couple of lines from that book you're carrying? In a low voice, Sally."

"Of course, poor boy," she replied and walked ten paces away and read me a couple of lines in a low voice. I heard every word.

"Come back," I said. I looked deep into her eyes when she returned, and I could find no guile in them. This girl was obviously on the level. "You say the boys would have been disappointed if you had refused. Is that right?"

She nodded.

I nodded.

"How does your head feel now, poor boy?"

"Sally, what time do your dates usually call for you?"

"Seven o'clock. But you come about fifteen minutes early so you can learn the rules before the others get there."

"I see," I said. "The rules."

"I'd tell you the rules now, only I'm late for class. It there anything I can do for you before I leave?"

I shook my head.

"I live off campus with my folks. The address is 1426 Ashland. See you tonight. Goodbye, poor boy."

She left me mumbling thickly.

Thinking about it all afternoon provided no solution. At 6:45 I stood on Sally's stoop with a puzzled expression and a dozen American Beauties. Sally answered the door. "How is your head, poor boy?" she asked as she led me into the living room.

"Fine," I answered, looking cautiously about me. Everything seemed to be in order. It was a tastefully decorated room with the usual furniture and appointments. On a divan flanking the fireplace sat a handsome man and woman who appeared to be in their middle forties.

"Mother, Dad," said Sally, "this is Dobie Gillis, the boy I was telling you about."

"How is your head, poor boy?" said Mrs. Bean.

"Fine," I said.

Mr. Bean rose and extended his hand. I reached out to shake it, but instead he took the bouquet of flowers from my other hand.

"That is the first rule, Dobie," he said. "No flowers, no candy, no perfume, no gifts of any kind. And, most particularly, no letters or phone calls."

"Sally," said Mrs. Bean reproachfully, "you should have told Dobie."

"I'm sorry, Mother. I had to rush to class."

"Won't you sit down, Dobie?" said Mrs. Bean. "Mr. Bean will explain the rules."

I fell heavily into a chair. "Please," I begged.

"It's really very simple," said Mr. Bean. "Will you have a cigarette?"

I shook my head dumbly.

He lighted a cigarette, sat down beside his wife, and began. "As you can see, Dobie, Sally is a very attractive girl. I think it is safe to say that she will find a young man without difficulty."

That, at least, made sense. I nodded enthusiastically.

"Sally," he went on, "is also a very tender-hearted girl. She is greatly disturbed by suffering. She will go to great lengths to help out anybody who is in trouble or in pain. She inherits this admirable quality from her mother."

A tender glance passed between husband and wife.

"To illustrate my point, Dobie," he said, "this afternoon when you bumped your head——"

"How is your head, poor boy?" asked Sally and her mother in tandem.

"Fine," I said.

"As I was saying, this afternoon when you bumped your

head, Sally would have done anything to make you feel better. If you had asked her to go steady, or even to marry you, it is very likely that she would have accepted."

"*Now* he tells me," I muttered.

"As you can see, Dobie," he continued, "Sally's tender heart is a bit of a problem. When she was a little girl, it wasn't so serious. But now that she is of an age to go steady, or to get married, for that matter, the situation is downright dangerous. For example, what if you had asked Sally to marry you this afternoon? I mean no offense, Dobie. I'm sure you're a fine, upstanding young man. But what if you were not? What if you were a cad and Sally had agreed to marry you? Her whole life would be ruined."

Mrs. Bean patted her husband's hand. "She might not have been as lucky as I was."

"Mother and Dad met in an elevator in a department store," Sally explained. "Her hatpin stuck in his cheek and twelve hours later they were married."

"All right," I allowed. "It's a dangerous situation. I see where Sally's tender heart could get her into all kinds of trouble. But what about the rules?"

"I'm coming to that," said Mr. Bean. "When Sally was old enough to start having dates, it was clear that she needed some kind of protection. We couldn't keep her locked in the house. At the same time we couldn't run the risk of letting some unscrupulous young man get her alone and force her into marriage by playing on her sympathies. So we sat down, Sally and her mother and I, and we arrived at a solution. We agreed, all three of us, that she would never have dates with one boy at a time. When she went out, she would go with several boys, no one of whom would be allowed to spend any time with her alone, to send her gifts or letters, to call her on the phone, or otherwise to gain any advantage over the others."

There was no mystery any more. "Safety in numbers," I said.

"Precisely."

I thought for a moment. "What's to prevent somebody from getting Sally alone during the day when she's at school—as I did this afternoon?"

"She only talked to you today because you had hurt yourself. If you hadn't bumped your head, if you had just come up to her and tried to start a conversation, she would have walked away."

I looked questioningly at Sally. She nodded affirmation.

"You mean," I asked her father, "that Sally isn't allowed to talk to men on campus?"

"Oh, certainly," he said. "As long as it's casual—about schoolwork or things like that. But if the conversation takes a romantic turn, she leaves immediately. That's one of the rules."

"What if a man breaks the rules?"

"Then he is disqualified and Sally won't see him any more."

All the loopholes seemed to be closed. "How long has this been going on?" I asked.

"Since Sally was sixteen. Two years."

"And how much longer will it go on?" I asked the question nervously. I did not look forward to becoming a member of a convoy for Sally. Perhaps I could stand it for a short while, but if it dragged on for any length of time I feared my love for her would drive me mad. It would have been different if I were a stronger man; then if things became intolerable, I could truss her in a sack and carry her off to the tall timber. But with my meager physique that was not possible.

"How much longer it goes on depends on Sally," replied her father. "The day she comes home and tells us that she is honestly in love with some young man—someone she has picked entirely on his merits and not out of sympathy—we will gladly suspend the rules. She's old enough now to know her own mind—provided she is allowed to make it up freely."

"Sally," I said, turning to her, "I hope that when you finally do choose a man, you won't make the mistake of

picking an athlete. As everyone knows, they make no-
toriously bad husbands. Now a small, weak man, on the
other hand——"

"Dobie," interrupted Mr. Bean, quickly changing the
subject, "what are you studying at school?"

"Journalism."

"That sounds keen," said Sally. "I'm taking home economics."

"There now," I cried, "is my idea of a perfect marriage—a journalist and a home economist. While he is
out reporting, she is home economizing."

"I hear somebody at the door," said Mr. Bean grate-
fully.

"I'll go," said Sally. She returned in a moment with
a male quartet. They said good evening to Mr. and Mrs.
Bean and circled me warily. I noted with sinking heart
that they were all great, strapping fellows. Sally made the
introductions—Davy Ball, Georgie Packer, Bob Sindorf,
Ellis Ford—and they squashed my puny hand in turn.

"Somebody's missing," said Sally. "Where's Joe Brack-
en?"

"He said to tell you he's not coming any more," said
Georgie. "He said it's been grand but he's decided to try
to find a girl he can have all to himself."

"I hope he does," said Sally sincerely. "He's a nice boy."

She got her coat. I stepped forward to help her put it
on, but I was flung into a corner by Bob. "My turn tonight," he snarled.

"Well, let's get going," said Ellis. They threw a cordon
around her and escorted her out of the house, I scamp-
ering around the edges like the odd pig in a litter.

A car stood outside. "Front going, back coming," said
Sally. They nodded. She got into the front seat between
Davy and Ellis. The rest of us got in back. "I'll sit in the
back on the way home, Dobie," she explained to me.

"Splendid," I muttered.

The car pulled out from the curb. "I ran ninety-eight
yards for a touchdown this afternoon," said Davy.

"Oo, marvy," said Sally.

"I shot twenty-four baskets last night," said Ellis.

"That's super," said Sally.

"I tied the Olympic record for the hammer throw yesterday," said Bob.

"Golly Moses," said Sally.

"I pitched a no-hit game last summer," said Georgie.

"Hey, groovy," said Sally.

I cleared my throat. "I can float on my back," I said.

"I'm hungry," said Sally. "Will we be at the restaurant soon?"

"Here it is now," said Davy.

We parked and went inside. Georgie pulled out Sally's chair, Bob helped her off with her coat, Ellis handed her a menu, and Davy relayed her order to the waiter. When dinner came, Ellis passed her the salt, Davy passed her the pepper, Bob the rolls, and Georgie the butter.

I sat hunched over my calves' liver, eating without tasting, crushed, defeated, hopeless. I was licked; I didn't have a chance. All at once I could stand it no longer.

"Excuse me," I said, rising. "I think I'll go home. I don't feel well."

"Oh, you poor boy," cried Sally, bounding from her chair and rushing over to me. "You poor, poor boy. What can I do to help?"

Suddenly hope was reborn. There was a way to get Sally. I went instantly into action. "It's ptomaine," I gasped and fell writhing to the floor.

"My baby," shrieked Sally. "My poor baby." She fell to her knees and stroked me wildly about the head and shoulders.

"I got it too," yelled Georgie and hurled himself to the floor.

"Me too," cried the others, and in a moment they were all thrashing about, groaning mightily, upsetting tables as they heaved their great bodies around the floor. Sally ran from one to the other. The manager followed her, wringing his hands. "Please, lady, make 'em stop," he begged. "They'll ruin my business."

"You poor man," said Sally, pausing in her rounds to stroke the manager.

"Ah, nuts," I mumbled. I rose and brushed myself off. The others lay still, watching me intently.

"Are you better, poor boy?" asked Sally.

"I am if they are," I replied with a nod toward the fallen four.

They picked themselves up. "Yeah, we're all right now," said Georgie.

"Thank heaven," breathed Sally.

"Maybe you better go home, Dobie," said Ellis.

"I'll see you to the door," said Bob, grasping me in a wristlock and hustling me out. He put me on the sidewalk and said, "You ever try that again and I'll knock your head down into your rib cage."

"Oh yeah?" I said when he had gone back into the restaurant.

I went to my room and beat the pillow until my little fists were red. Bilked, outwitted, bypassed. And nothing could be done about it. I pitched and tossed until dawn.

Calm came with the early morning light. I went over the problem slowly and rationally. One thing was obvious: I had no chance to win Sally in open competition with the other suitors. Not that she was an athlete worshiper; I felt sure that she would really prefer a man of my intellectual attainments. But how could I make an impression on her with all those huge, towering fellows blocking me off from her view? No, I was lost unless I could attack her vulnerable point—her tender heart.

But in order to do that effectively, I had to get her alone. If I tried appealing to her sympathy with the others around, the same thing would happen that happened last night—plus Bob would knock my head down into my rib cage. And the others were always around, except, of course, while Sally was at school during the day. But that was no good either. If I tried to talk to her on campus I had to—according to the rules—keep the conversation casual, discuss schoolwork or something innocuous.

For a moment I toyed with the idea of going around campus banging my head into statues on the chance that she would find me again. But I abandoned the idea shortly; I didn't have the stamina for it.

Clearly I was licked. I was at the bottom of a black pit of despondency when I was suddenly exploded out by a great, brilliant, bursting idea.

What if Sally transferred from home economics to journalism? What if we were together all day long in classes? Sure, I would abide by the rules; I would confine the conversation to schoolwork. But we would be together all day—that was the important thing. She could not help but notice me, assess my true worth, and be impressed. Particularly in journalism. Remember, I had had years of newspaper experience. I knew the jargon, the techniques, the complicated ins-and-outs of reporting. Sally, still struggling with the A B Cs of journalism, would be awed at my professionalism, and the awe would inevitably ripen into love, and she would go home and tell her parents to suspend the rules, for she had found her man.

I leaped from my bed with a bellow of joy. There would be no trouble, I knew, in persuading Sally to transfer to journalism. Once I described the glamour and romance of the profession to her, how could she resist it?

I was waiting outside the home economics building when Sally arrived for her first class. "Good morning, Sally," I cried cheerily.

"Good morning," she said. "You know that we can't talk about anything but schoolwork, don't you, Dobie?"

"Of course. That's exactly what I want to talk about. Sit down." I drew her to the steps beside me. "Sally, have you ever thought of switching to journalism?"

"Why, no."

"Well, you should. There's a great future in it for women. Look at Inez Robb, Anne O'Hare McCormick, Marguerite Higgins, Martha Gellhorn, Rebecca West. They travel all over the world, meet all kinds of people. Adventure! Intrigue! Excitement!"

"I don't want to go anywhere," said Sally.

"Oh," I said, taken aback, but only for a moment.
"That's all right. You don't have to go anywhere. You
can get to be a big newspaperwoman right here in this
country. Look at Dorothy Kilgallen, May Craig, Elsie
Robinson. Millions of readers! Big salaries! Prestige!"

"Gee, I'd be scared."

"Nonsense. You'd love it. The roar of the press! The
bustle of the city room! The smell of printer's ink!"

"I'm allergic to printer's ink."

"Well, you don't actually smell it. It's just a figure of
speech. Really, Sally, you'd love it. You get a press card
and you can go through police lines, see fires and riots
and all kinds of wonderful disasters."

"Not me, Dobie. Disasters upset me."

I was getting desperate. "You don't have to cover disasters necessarily. You could be a society reporter, go to
big fancy weddings."

"I don't like big weddings. I like little ones with just
the families and maybe a few intimate friends and a tenor
singing 'I Love You Truly.' "

"That's fine, Sally. You could go to *little* weddings.
Thousands of 'em."

She shook her head. "I don't think little weddings
should have strangers at them."

"All right," I said hoarsely. "Don't go to weddings. Be
a drama critic."

"They're mean."

"Write editorials, then. Or sell ads. Or read copy.
There's a million things you could do on a newspaper."

"I don't think so, Dobie. I'm crazy about home economics and I want to stay with it."

"Think it over," I pleaded. "Won't you at least think it
over?"

"What for? I'm perfectly satisfied with home economics."

Perspiration was cascading off my forehead. "How
about trying journalism for just one semester? I'm sure
you'll love it."

"I'm sure I won't, Dobie." She rose from the steps. "I've got to hurry to class now."

I reached up and seized her hand. "You're absolutely sure you don't want to transfer to journalism?"

"Absolutely."

"And that's final?" I asked forlornly.

"And that's final." She freed her hand and went into the building.

There was only one other thing I could do. And I did it.

It worked fine. By the end of our freshman year we were going steady. We got engaged in our senior year and married the day after commencement. We've got a nice little restaurant in Minneapolis now—Dobie's and Sally's —and business is improving all the time. It's not hard to understand why. Nobody else in town serves meals so attractive and nutritious at such a low price. Believe me, that stuff I learned in home economics comes in mighty handy.

Love of Two Chemists

I am sometimes asked, "How come you took chemistry?" and I reply, "How come Leander swam the Hellespont?" For the answer is the same: a woman.

A woman drove me to chemistry; nothing else. Certainly it was not my natural inclination. My natural inclination is not toward chemistry; it is, however, toward women.

It must not be thought that I am a rake. With me the pursuit of women is only part of a much larger plan—the pursuit of pleasure. I am a hedonist.

I became a practitioner of hedonism quite by chance a few years ago when I happened to run across the word in the dictionary. "Hedonism," it said. "The doctrine that pleasure is the sole or chief good in life. The leading advocates of Hedonism in antiquity were the Epicureans and the Cyrenaics."

I can't tell you how happy I was to find this definition. I had long believed that pleasure was the sole or chief good in life, but this was the first time I knew that it was a *doctrine*. Many people, notably my father, had been calling me a bum and, to tell the truth, I had had to agree with them. But learning about the Epicureans and the

Cyrenaics put everything in a new light. One would hardly call an Epicurean a bum, and surely not a Cyrenaic.

Bolstered by the knowledge that I was following an ancient and honorable doctrine, I plunged with renewed vigor into the pursuit of pleasure. When people, notably my father, still called me a bum, I would only smile inscrutably and say, "Ha! That's all you know about it."

So much for hedonism. Now to get back to the woman who drove me to chemistry. Her name was Helen Frith. She was sixteen years old, actually a little too young for me. I prefer women closer to my own age, which is eighteen. In view, however, of her extravagant development, I was willing to stretch a point. She stood five feet four inches tall in her dirty saddle shoes. Her weight, as nearly as I could decently ascertain, was 110 pounds. Her hair was the color of honey produced by real bees. Her eyes were a smoky gray. (I refer, of course, to the irises; the rest of the eyeball was white.) Her nose was short and symmetrical; her lips full, soft, and red. Her teeth were even and free from caries. Her skin was as good as skin gets. Her figure had no unsightly bulges, but several sightly ones.

I first encountered this phantom of delight during freshman registration. This was for me a time of confusion. I was supposed to be making out a program for my freshman year. I stood in a line with several hundred other freshmen, moving slowly toward the desk of the faculty adviser. When I reached the desk, I was to tell the adviser what courses I wanted to take and, with his assistance, make out my program. But I didn't know what courses I wanted to take. Looking over the curriculum, I saw absolutely nothing that would appeal to a hedonist. Still, I had to take *something*. My father had been quite insistent on that point.

The line moved forward, and I began to grow panicky. A horrible vision of myself working in my father's bakery popped into my mind. That was the dire punishment he had promised me if I did not make a success of college. In fact, he had wanted me to work in the bakery instead of going to college in the first place. It had taken many days of passionate oratory to change his mind.

And now I was getting closer and closer to the desk of the adviser, still without an inkling of what I wanted to take. I rummaged wildly through the catalogue of courses, but I finally gave it up in despair. Let the adviser advise me, I thought. That's what he's there for.

Mr. McCandless, the adviser, was a man in his early thirties. He had not been a teacher long enough to develop the deep hatred of students that characterize older members of the faculty. He greeted me with a pleasant smile and asked my name.

"Dobie Gillis," I confessed.

"And what would you like to take?" he asked.

"I don't rightly know," I replied.

"What are you interested in chiefly?" he asked.

"Women," I replied.

"Maybe you'd like to study gynecology," he suggested.

"No," I said, "I'm not *that* interested."

"Well, how about history or economics?"

"Neh," I said.

"Anthropology? Sociology? Psychology?"

"Neh."

"How about the sciences—chemistry, maybe."

"There is nothing that appeals to me quite so little as chemistry."

Law, journalism, philosophy, physical education, geology, languages, zoology, archaeology, pharmacy, civil engineering, mechanical engineering, electrical engineering, and aeronautical engineering failed likewise to excite me.

"Look," said Mr. McCandless hoarsely, "why don't you just step aside and think for a few minutes while I take care of the other people in this line?"

So I stepped aside and the student behind me came up to the desk. The student behind me was the Helen Frith described above.

I am a man who under normal circumstances can keep his emotion perfectly concealed. But the first sight of Miss

Helen Frith was by no means a normal circumstance. I felt my eyes bug, my jaw drop, and my kneecaps leap like hares. I tried vainly to compose myself. All I could do was to clutch the corner of the desk and blink rapidly at her.

Mr. McCandless looked at me with some nervousness, but Helen Frith seemed not to notice. "I am Helen Frith," she said in a forthright soprano, "and I want to take chemistry."

"Just a moment, miss," said Mr. McCandless. He turned to me. "You all right, Gillis?"

I nodded dumbly.

"I," continued Helen Frith, "want to be a great chemist and make simply marvelous discoveries. I want to find cures for diseases and also formulae that will increase crop yields, aid industry, eliminate pests, and make life richer and fuller for all the peoples of the earth."

"And so do I!" I cried, waving a clenched fist in the air.

Mr. McCandless gaped at me. "What's going on here?" he demanded. "A minute ago you said nothing appealed to you less than chemistry."

"A minute ago it was true," I replied. "But this young lady has opened my eyes." I grasped her hand in both of mine. "Miss Frith, may I say what's in my heart?" I asked.

"Please do," she said with a warm smile.

"Scarcely a moment ago," I said, "I was a man without a purpose, a ship without a rudder. But you have shown me the way. I know what I want. I want to take chemistry with you, make discoveries with you, lighten mankind's burden with you. You and I together, test tubes in hand, from this day forward!"

"Gee," she said. "Just like Marie and Pierre Curie."

"Precisely," I agreed. "You must call me Pierre and I will call you Marie."

"Pierre," she breathed.

"Marie," I breathed.

We stood clasped silently, lost in the magic of the moment.

"There is a university policy," said Mr. McCandless

severely, "about undergraduates embracing in scholastic buildings."

I released Helen—Marie, I mean—and Mr. McCandless made out our programs. Then we went over to the Kozy Kampus Korner to get better acquainted.

There, over two Varsity Vooms (one scoop vanilla, one scoop chocolate, one scoop coleslaw, hot fudge, and rolled anchovies), I learned that chemistry had not always been the driving force in Marie's life. It was, in fact, only a recent preoccupation. In previous years she had embraced numerous other causes. At age twelve she had been a militant suffragette. This came to an abrupt end when she found out that women already had the vote. The following year she took up yoga exercises and practiced them with great fidelity. These she gave up at her mother's earnest entreaties when her biceps got somewhat larger than Rocky Graziano's. It took a year of enforced indolence to make her arms girlish again. Later there were, successively, bird-walking, playing the timpani, vegetarianism, and arrowhead collecting, all of which palled in their turn. Now it was chemistry.

My heart went out to her as I listened. All her life the poor girl had been seeking, groping, striving for her proper niche. Now she thought that chemistry was the answer, but one look at her and I could tell that it was not. She would soon tire of chemistry and embark once more on her endless quest for fulfillment, only to find disappointment again.

Had our paths not crossed, I thought, she might have spent her whole life in this feckless search. But I knew what she wanted. I knew the one pursuit, the one cause, that would bring her the genuine, soul-deep satisfaction that had so long eluded her. I refer, of course, to hedonism.

For it was obvious to my practiced eye that this girl was made for hedonism. The eagerness of her, the bubbling enthusiasm, the way she walked and talked and smiled— all these were indications that could not be misinterpreted. Beyond cavil she was meant to be a hedonist.

And my heart sang with the joy of this knowledge. Already I could see the two of us in pursuit of pleasure— dancing together, tobogganing together, roasting frank- furters together, seeing movies together, just *being* to- gether. I could scarcely confine my enthusiasm. Practicing hedonism alone, as I had been, was well enough, but a hedonist without a mate is really only half a hedonist.

I was about to start converting her when I was struck by a sobering thought: it was too soon. Hedonism re- quired complete concentration, and right now her mind was filled with all that chemistry nonsense. Better to wait until she tired of chemistry before I began my missionary work; certainly it would not be very long.

In the meantime, while chemistry was her preoccupa- tion, I would string along. I would do better; I would pretend to match her enthusiasm for the subject. In this way I would persuade her that we were truly soulmates and make it easier to sell hedonism to her later.

So I took her to the Knoll, the campus trysting place, and there we sat under a fine old oak, her head on my shoulder, her hand in mine, and for six unbroken hours we talked of finding cures for cancer, leukemia, elm blight, and the discoloration of chocolate in hot weather.

Classes began the following morning. My first glimpse of chemistry lab filled me with foreboding. It was all so grim and scientific, and I am so ungrim and unscientific. I shuddered as I looked at the row on row of high work- tables, each littered with a terrifying assortment of beak- ers and vials and flasks and test tubes and Bunsen burners. Were it not for the comforting sight of Marie at the next table, somehow looking chic in a rubber lab apron, I would have bolted immediately.

After the class was assembled, two men in white smocks walked in. One was tall and crotchety-looking. The other was short and crotchety-looking. The tall one stepped to the lectern at the front of the class. The short one took a chair over at one side.

"This class is called Fundamentals of Chemistry," said the tall one to the students. "I am Mr. Fitzhugh. That"—

he nodded to the short one—"is Mr. Obispo. I do the lecturing. Mr. Obispo supervises the lab work.

"You are all freshmen," continued Mr. Fitzhugh, "and
you may not be familiar with the term 'pipe course.' A
pipe course is a course where students can get passing
grades without doing much work. This is *not* a pipe
course. You have never worked as hard in your lives as
you are going to work here. If any of you is looking for
something easy, I'd advise you to leave now."

I looked longingly at the door.

"This course," said Mr. Fitzhugh, "is dedicated to the
idiotic proposition that you can be taught the fundamentals of organic chemistry, inorganic chemistry, quali-
tative analysis, quantitative analysis, physical chemistry,
and biochemistry all in one semester. The odds against
any of you passing this course would be staggering to con-
template if there were any time for contemplation. However, there is not. Get out your notebooks."

I think I was moaning aloud, because several students
turned to look at me. What had I gotten myself into? All
I needed was one flunk to end up in my father's bakery,
and if I was ever face to face with a flunk, this was it. My
nostrils were suddenly filled with the smell of baking
bread. I gathered up my books. I was getting out even if
it meant losing Marie. Then I looked at her sitting at the
next table with her pencil poised over her notebook, her
face flushed, her eyes shining, the tip of her pretty pink
tongue sticking out of the side of her mouth in concentration, and my bones turned to water. I couldn't leave
her. I just couldn't. Heaving a mighty sigh, I put down
my books and got ready to take notes.

For the next hour Mr. Fitzhugh, speaking a little faster
than Clem McCarthy when he is announcing the Ken-
tucky Derby, delivered a lecture about matter, elements,
mixtures, compounds, reagents, the periodic table, atomic
weights, ionization, valence, and other improbable topics.
At the end of the hour I had nineteen pages of notes, all
illegible.

After class at the Kozy Kampus Korner Marie was brim-

ming with joy. "Isn't it wonderful, Pierre?" she gushed.
"All that work, work, work. And there'll be more. Oh, the
chemist's life is a busy one."

"Yeah," I mumbled, toying dejectedly with my Freshman Frappé (lemon sherbet, grenadine, and diced lamb).

She noticed my funk. "I know it may seem a little bor-
ing at first," she said sympathetically. "I mean just taking
lecture notes isn't very exciting. But wait till we start lab
work." Her eyes grew dreamy. "Mixing stuff in test tubes
and burning things and pouring things . . . Wow-dow!"
she cried in a transport of delight.

Lab work began the following week. First Mr. Fitzhugh
explained the experiment. We were each to put three
grams of red mercuric oxide in a test tube, connect it to a
water trough by means of a bent glass tube, and heat the
mercuric oxide with a Bunsen burner until bubbles rose
from the water trough into a gas bottle above it. The gas
that bubbled up, said Mr. Fitzhugh, would be oxygen.
"See that the bubble don't come up too fast," he cautioned.

We all started working while Mr. Obispo, the lab as-
sistant, circulated among us. "Watch those bubbles," he
kept warning.

I must confess that I rather enjoyed this first experiment, but my enjoyment was as nothing compared to
Marie's. She was beside herself with rapture. "Look, look,
look!" she squealed as the mercuric oxide changed color.
"Bubbles!" she shrieked as the bubbles started to rise in
her water trough. "Look how fast they're coming! Oh,
Pierre, isn't it marvy? Oh, look, look, they're coming faster
now. And still faster! And still fas——"

Her last observation was interrupted as her gas bottle
exploded, sending a spray of water and glass shards to
the ceiling ten feet above.

Mr. Obispo materialized behind Marie, an expression
of great pain on his face. "Little girl," he said, "perhaps
you ought to transfer to home economics. You can't hurt
yourself with fudge."

Marie bridled, but said nothing. After class, however,

she confessed to me that she thought Mr. Obispo was icky.

Her opinion of Mr. Obispo deteriorated progressively in succeeding weeks as he made comment on her destruction of various tubes, retorts, beakers, burettes, funnels, pipettes, pestles, Liebig condensers, and Erlenmeyer flasks. Marie's trouble was twofold. First she had a notable lack of manual dexterity. Second, and more important, the sight of chemicals changing color and fluids bubbling would make her take leave of her senses. She would become powerless with delight. She would stand transfixed, breathing heavily through parted lips, until the crash of breaking glass brought her out of her trance. It got so all the students in her vicinity moved to other tables—except me, of course. Such was the greatness of my love.

Mr. Obispo's reactions evolved from heavy sarcasm through genuine annoyance to black rage. The day she broke seven jars, six delivery tubes, and a Florence flask in a single chlorine-making experiment, he was near apoplexy. He called her a murderess that day.

I was pleased with the way things were going. I knew that if her breakage continued at its current rate—and there was no reason to suppose it would not—her attachment for chemistry would soon be over. Mr. Obispo's outbursts were making her more and more miserable, and before long I knew she would be at the end of her tether. Or if that didn't happen, her father would eventually cool her enthusiasm for chemistry. She had to keep writing home for more money to pay for all the things she broke, and the old boy was getting livid.

In any case, her infatuation with chemistry could not last much longer, and nobody would be happier than I when it ended. The combination of Mr. Obispo's experiments and Mr. Fitzhugh's lectures was making me old before my time. Mr. Fitzhugh had not exaggerated when he promised us that we would work harder than we ever had in our lives.

The great day finally came around the middle of the semester. Marie broke a carboy that day. Nobody in the long history of the university had ever broken a carboy.

Even at Dupont, I understand, where thousands of car-
boys are handled daily, it is a rare event. It is by no
means easy to break a carboy; they stand as high as a
man's waist and their glass is like steel. But Marie did it.

Obispo turned white, then red, then purple, then white
again. He hopped on one leg, then the other, then both.
For upwards of five minutes only strangled sounds came
from his throat. Then he found his tongue and with it
delivered an oration on Marie's unfitness for chemistry,
for college in general, and for the human race as a whole.
At length he collapsed in the corner in a twitching heap.

Marie was pretty broken up herself and I took her to
the Knoll to comfort her. She sobbed for a spell while I
drummed sympathetically on her shoulder blades. Then
she composed herself. "Pierre," she said, averting her eyes
from mine, "you'll hate me for this."

"I couldn't hate you," I said truthfully and gave her a
squeeze as an earnest.

"I've failed you," she said miserably. "You wanted for
us to be great chemists together, but I can't, Pierre. I'm
through with chemistry. You'll have to go on alone."

"No," I said stoutly. "We'll find something we can do
together."

"I can't let you, Pierre. I know how badly you want to
be a chemist."

"It would be meaningless without you."

"But could you be happy doing anything else?"

"You," I said in a voice husky with tenderness, "are
my happiness."

"And you'd give up chemistry for me?"

"Yes," I said simply.

She vaulted into my arms. "Oh, Pierre!" she cried.

I fondled her for a longish interval and then I sprang
my trap. It was like taking candy from a baby. It was like
shooting fish in a barrel. It was easy as pie. Nobody was
ever converted to hedonism more readily than Marie.

In fact, she wanted to become an all-out hedonist right
away. She was for immediately giving up everything that
we didn't like—chemistry specifically—and throwing our-

selves without delay into the full-time pursuit of pleasure. Mindful of my father's bakery, I persuaded her that we should complete the semester in chemistry. "Next semester," I told her, "we'll choose all pipe courses that won't interfere with our hedonism. But for now we'll have to continue with chemistry. Of course, we don't have to go to class as often as we have been. We can cut it occasionally."

And, truly, I meant to cut chemistry only occasionally. But once we started hedonizing, it became more and more inconvenient to go to classes. In a very short time, we were not cutting class occasionally, we were *attending* occasionally.

I worried about it sometimes. I would get a sudden vision of flunking chemistry, being yanked out of college and stuck in my father's bakery. But this disquieting thought did not come often. I was too happy to worry. The joys of hedonism simply blotted out unpleasant thinking. There were too many blessings to count.

The first blessing was that we didn't have to call one another Marie and Pierre any more. This was a great boon because we had quite forgotten our real names in the preceding weeks. I had had to look in my wallet whenever somebody asked my name. It was worse for her; she didn't carry a wallet.

Now, properly identified as Helen Frith and Dobie Gillis, we embarked on an excruciatingly pleasurable program of movies, dancing, skiing, skating, tobogganing, smooching, and allied pursuits. We laughed and played the livelong day; we whooped and hollered; we pranced and cavorted; we leaped and spun; we drank the headiest draughts that life offered.

One Friday morning—it was sleeting and really too cold for outdoor activity—we decided to drop in on our chemistry class. Mr. Obispo greeted us with elaborate courtesy. "So nice," he said, " to see you after all these weeks."

"Nice to be here," I replied politely.

"What's this bottle for?" asked Helen, pointing at a tightly corked brown bottle on her table. A label on the bottle said SOLUTION K. On my table was a similar bottle labeled SOLUTION L.

"During your long absence," said Mr. Obispo pleasantly, "each member of the class was given an unidentified solution. You are supposed to analyze your solution and turn in a report on its contents."

"How do you analyze a solution?" I asked in honest ignorance.

"Mr. Fitzhugh explained the process in some detail while you were gone," he replied, still smiling.

"When are our reports due?" asked Helen nervously.

Mr. Obispo's smile broadened. "First thing Monday morning."

We blanched. Here it was Friday, and the reports were due Monday morning. That meant we had only two sessions to make our analysis—today's and Saturday's. And we didn't have the vaguest idea how to make an analysis.

"Tell me," I said in a frantic treble, "how long does it take to analyze this stuff?"

Mr. Obispo beamed. "That depends on your grasp of the technique. Most of the students have been working on their solutions for two weeks. Of course, it can be done in a shorter time—say ten days, or even eight days if the student is exceptionally talented."

"I suppose," I said in a dry croak, "that you flunk the course if you don't turn in your report on time."

"Right," he answered cheerily. "Well, I'll be moving along now. I don't want to keep you from your work." He started away and then turned. "Oh, incidentally, in case you were entertaining a notion of copying somebody else's report, I think I should tell you that each student has a different solution." With a merry wave, he walked away.

"Oh, Dobie, what'll we do?" wailed Helen.

"The important thing is to keep our heads," I said, although I didn't know what I would do with mine even if I kept it. It contained not one iota of information about chemical analysis.

"How are we ever going to find out how to do this stuff?" she cried in anguish.

"We'll borrow somebody's lecture notes," I said. "You ask the kids on this side of the room, I'll take the other."

Rapidly we canvassed the whole class in the hope that somebody would lend us his lecture notes. It was no use. Everybody was still working on his solution and needed his notes. We returned to our tables and sat staring gloomily at our solutions until the bell rang. Mr. Obispo cast us a delighted smile from time to time.

After class we went to the Kozy Kampus Korner and examined our problem in all its aspects. After several dark, unfruitful hours an answer finally came to me. It was a desperate answer, but so was our problem.

"Listen, Helen," I said. "Tomorrow is Saturday. The chemistry class is over at noon. There are no classes Saturday afternoon. There are also no classes on Sunday. The chemistry building is locked from Saturday noon until Monday morning."

"So?"

"So at the end of class tomorrow morning, we'll borrow somebody's lecture notes. They'll all be finished with their analysis tomorrow so there won't be any trouble borrowing the notes. Then when the class files out of the room tomorrow, you and I will duck into the broom closet and close the door. If you recall, there's a broom closet right across the aisle from my desk."

"What'll we do in the broom closet?"

"We'll hide in there until we're sure Obispo and Fitzhugh and the janitor and everybody has left the building. Then we'll come out and go to work on the analysis. We'll work right straight through until Monday morning. We'll bring flashlights so we can work at night too."

"Why can't we turn on the lights?"

"Somebody might see. There's a very strict university rule about students staying in classrooms after hours without chaperones—especially students of mixed sexes."

Helen grinned suddenly. "You know, Dobie, this sounds kind of exciting. I mean danger and adventure and intrigue and all that stuff. I bet it's going to be fun."

"Sure," I said. It hadn't occurred to me as fun before, but now I could see the possibilities. "Tell you what. Let's bring sandwiches and make a kind of picnic out of it."

"And pickles too," said Helen. "I love pickles."

"All right. One of us will bring sandwiches and the other one will bring pickles. Now let's go over our plans carefully so there won't be any hitch."

There was no hitch. The following morning, just before the class ended, we approached a couple of students for their lecture notes and they turned them over without argument. Then when the bell rang and the students started filing out, we gathered up our things and ducked into the broom closet. Unseen, we closed the door behind us. We huddled cheek by jowl in the darkness.

We heard Mr. Fitzhugh and Mr. Obispo making preparations to leave. "Say, Obispo," said Fitzhugh, "maybe we ought to hang around and get that potassium sulfate ready for Monday morning's experiment. It'll only take a couple of hours."

My heart sank. Asphyxiation in our present situation was no improbability.

"I can't," replied Mr. Obispo, to my immense relief. "I promised the wife I'd take her downtown to look at some dresses this afternoon."

"How can she buy dresses on your salary?" asked Mr. Fitzhugh.

"She can't," answered Mr. Obispo. "She just likes to look at them."

"We've got to get that potassium ready before class on Monday," said Mr. Fitzhugh.

"We can get here early Monday morning and do it," said Mr. Obispo.

Mr. Fitzhugh agreed and they left. We stayed in the closet for another half hour while the janitor came in and cleaned up the lab. Only after we heard the janitor's footsteps going downstairs and the sound of the outside door being locked did we emerge.

"Kind of scary, isn't it?" said Helen, and indeed the empty lab did look sinister.

"We won't notice it after we start working," I assured her.

"Let's eat first, Dobie. I'm hungry."

"All right." I opened a bag and took out a quart jar. "Here are the pickles."

Her jaw dropped. "Did you," she asked weakly, "bring pickles?"

"Sure. Why, what's wrong?"

She opened a bag and took out a quart jar. "I brought pickles too."

"No sandwiches?" I said in dismay.

"I thought you were bringing them."

"And I thought you were."

"That's all right," she said bravely. "I love pickles."

"Me too," I said with a grisly smile.

We sat down and ate pickles until our mouths puckered and then we went to work. First we read our lecture notes. Helen frankly confessed herself baffled. So was I, although, for the sake of her morale, I didn't admit it. "We'll get the hang of it once we're started," I kept saying.

"Well, let's get started then." She reached for a test tube.

I laid a restraining hand on her arm. "Helen," I said as kindly as possible, "I mean no offense, but I think I better do all the lab work. You know how you get when you're working with chemicals. We can't afford to have any explosions right now. It might attract people."

"Oh, all right," she said, pouting a little.

"I'll do your solution first and then I'll do mine. You read the notes to me as I work."

She picked up the notebook and started to read: "To test for metals of the hydrochloric acid group, add dilute hydrochloric acid with a constant stirring until a precipitate ceases to form. Allow the precipitate to settle and add a few more drops of acid to make sure the precipitation is complete. Decant the supernatant liquid through a filler, wash the residue twice by decantation, and finally transfer it to the filter. Treat the residue with 50 cc. of boiling water and return to the funnel at least three times. Add NH_4OH and let stand for at least five minutes. Remove the pinchcock and catch the filtrate in a beaker."

After some false starts—about two hundred—I completed this part of the analysis and discovered that lead nitrate was one ingredient of Helen's solution. It was now slightly after 6 P.M. and the light was failing. We pulled the shades, turned on our flashlights, had a pickle, and proceeded with the second part of the analysis—testing for metals of the hydrogen sulphide group. This was a process consisting of twenty fiendishly complicated steps. When I finished, I knew that antimony nitrate was another ingredient of the solution, and dawn was breaking.

If there is anything that will take the heart out of a man, it is a pickle for breakfast. But there was no choice. Overcoming fatigue, heartache, and nausea, I slugged forward with the analysis. I was getting better at it now, and it took me only three hours to find that zinc nitrate was a third ingredient.

Until dark I ran a battery of other tests on Helen's solution, none of which yielded a thing. "I've finished it," I said wearily. "Your solution contains lead nitrate, antimony nitrate, and zinc nitrate."

"Oh, Dobie, you're wonderful," she breathed. "Have a pickle."

"I'm not hungry," I said quickly. "Come on, let's get started on my solution."

"Couldn't we rest for just a minute first?" she asked. "Just a little catnap before we go ahead. I'm beat, Dobie."

So was I. "All right," I agreed. "We'll sit down on our stools and put our heads on the table for just a couple of minutes."

So we sat down on our stools and put our heads on the tables for just a couple of minutes and the next thing I knew, daylight was streaming in the windows.

I looked at my watch. *Seven o'clock!* I leaped up with a bellow of consternation. Class began at eight-thirty!

Rudely I shook Helen awake and I ripped the cork out of my bottle of solution. "Come on, come on, start reading those notes," I cried.

But before she could begin, there came the unmistakable sound of the outside door being opened downstairs. We stared at one another, biting our knuckles in horror. Then I sprang into action. Helen's table was littered with tubes and flasks and beakers and pickle jars. I opened the drawer beneath her table and threw everything in. Then I grabbed her, dragged her into the broom closet and closed the door.

We heard two people come into the lab—Mr. Fitzhugh and Mr. Obispo. I remembered then that they had made plans to come to class early on Monday to prepare potassium sulfate. Juxtaposed in the airless closet, we heard them moving about the lab. Then we heard footsteps very close to the closet door. We heard the footsteps stop right by our worktables. We heard the sound of sniffing. "Hey, Fitz," said Mr. Obispo's voice, "do you smell something around here?"

And I remembered that I had left the bottle of my solution standing open on my table. A wave of faintness engulfed me, and I would have toppled over had there been room in the closet.

The sound of Mr. Fitzhugh's footsteps approaching. The sound of him sniffing. "Smells like $C_2H_2O_2$ in a five per cent solution," said Mr. Fitzhugh.

"That's it all right," said Mr. Obispo. "But where's it coming from?"

"Come on, Obispo, let's get the potassium ready," said Mr. Fitzhugh impatiently. "We haven't got much time."

We heard them walking away. I squeezed Helen exultantly. With great difficulty I stifled a cry of joy. Now in my darkest hour a kind fate has succored me. $C_2H_2O_2$ in a five per cent solution! Now I knew what was in my bottle! Now I would pass chemistry! Now I wouldn't have to go to work in my father's bakery!

This narrative is being written in my father's bakery.

I work there now. I am not in college any more. Maybe next year I'll go back. I hope so. Helen promised to wait for me.

The reason I am not in college is that I flunked chemistry. Helen passed it. We stayed hidden in the closet that morning until the rest of the students started coming into the lab. Then we sneaked out and got behind our tables. Nobody saw us; nobody suspected that we had spent the week end in the lab. We quickly wrote out reports on the contents of our solutions and we turned them in when the rest of the class did. Helen's report was correct. Mine was not. $C_2H_2O_2$ in a five per cent solution was not what was in my bottle. I guess I'll never know what *was* in my bottle, but I have found out what $C_2H_2O_2$ in a five per cent solution is. It is vinegar. What Mr. Fitzhugh and Mr. Obispo smelled was the pickles.

The Face Is
Familiar But—

You can never tell. Citizens, you can never tell. Take the week end of May 18. From all indications it was going to be a dreamboat. Saturday night was the fraternity formal, and Sunday night Petey Burch was taking me to the Dr. Askit quiz broadcast. Every prospect pleased.

At 7:30 Saturday night I got into my rented tux and picked up my rented car. At 8:30 I called for my date and was told that she had come down with the measles at 7:30. So I shugged my rented shoulders, got into my rented car, and went to the dance alone.

I had taken my place in the stag line when Petey Burch rushed up to me, his face flushed with excitement. He waved a letter at me. "I've got it!" he cried. "Here's a letter from my parents saying I can join the Navy." Petey, like me, was seventeen years old and needed permission from home to enlist.

"That's swell, Petey," I said. "I've got some news too. My date has the measles."

"Tough," he said sympathetically. Then he suddenly got more excited than ever and hollered: "No! No, that's

perfect. Listen, Dobie, the recruiting station is still open.
I can go right down and enlist now."

"But what about the dance? What about your date?"

"The Navy," said Petey, snapping to attention, "needs
men *now*. Every minute counts. How can I think of staying at a dance when there's a war to be won? I've got to
get out of here, Dobie. I owe it to the boys Over There."

"What are you going to tell your date?"

"That's where you come in, Dobie. You take my girl; I
go catch a bus. I won't tell her anything. I'll just disappear and you explain it to her later."

"Won't she mind?"

"I suppose she will, but it doesn't really matter. This
is the first date I've ever had with her and I'll probably
never see her again." He set his jaw. "God knows when
I'll be coming back from Over There."

"I understand," I said simply.

"Thanks, old man," he said simply.

We shook hands.

"By the way," I said, "what about those two tickets
you've got for the Dr. Askit broadcast tomorrow night?"

"They're yours," he said, handing them to me.

"Thanks, old man," I said simply.

"Here comes my date now," Petey said, pointing at the
powder-room door. I took one look at her and knew what
a patriot he must be to run out on a smooth operator like
that. She was strictly on the side of angels.

"Where'd you find her?" I drooled.

"Just met her the other night. She's new around here.
Now. I'll introduce you and you dance with her while
I make my getaway."

"Solid," I agreed.

She walked over to us, making pink-taffeta noises. The
timing was perfect. The orchestra was tuning up for the
first number just as she reached us.

"Hi," said Petey. "I want you to meet a friend of mine.
Dobie Gillis, this is——"

At that instant the orchestra started to play and I didn't
catch her name. And no wonder. The orchestra was led

by a trumpeter who had a delusion that good trumpeting
and loud trumpeting are the same thing. Between him
and Harry James, he figured, were only a few hundred
decibels of volume. Every time he played he narrowed
the gap.

"Excuse me," shouted Petey, and left.

"Dance?" I yelled.

"What?" she screamed.

I made dancing motions and she nodded. We moved
out on the floor. I tried to tell her while we were dancing
that I hadn't caught her name, but it was impossible. The
trumpeter, feeling himself gaining on Harry James, was
pursuing his advantage hard. At last there came a short
trumpet break, and I made a determined stab at it.

"I don't like to seem dull," I said to the girl, "but when
Petey introduced us, I didn't catch your——"

But the trumpeter was back on the job, stronger than
ever after his little rest. The rest of the song made the
"Anvil Chorus" sound like a lullaby. I gave up then, and
we just danced.

Came the intermission and I tried again. "I know this
is going to sound silly, but when we were intro——"

"I wonder where Petey is," she interrupted. "He's been
gone an awfully long time."

"Oh, not so long really. Well, as I was saying, it makes
me feel foolish to ask, but I didn't——"

"It has, too, been a long time. I think that's an awfully
funny way for a boy to act when he takes a girl out for the
first time. Where do you suppose he is?"

"Oh, I don't know. Probably just—oh well, I suppose I
might as well tell you now." So I told her.

She bit her lip. "Dobie," she quavered, "will you please
take me home?"

"Home? It's so early."

"Please, Dobie."

Seventeen years of experience had taught me not to
argue with a woman whose eyes are full of tears. I went
and got my Driv-Ur-Self limousine, packed her into it,
and started off.

"I—live—at—2123—Fremont—Avenue," she wailed.

"There, there," I cooed. "Try to look at it his way. The Navy needs men *now*. The longer he stayed around the dance tonight, the longer the war would last. Believe me, if my parents would sign a letter for me, I'd be Over There plenty quick, believe me."

"You mean," she wept, "that you would run off and stand up a girl at a formal affair?"

"Well," I said, "maybe not that. I mean I would hardly run out on a girl like you." I took her hand. "A girl so beautiful and lovely and pretty."

She smiled through tears. "You're sweet, Dobie."

"Oh, pshaw," I pshawed. "Say, I've got a couple of tickets to the Dr. Askit quiz broadcast tomorrow night. How about it?"

"Oh, Dobie, I'd love to. Only I don't know if Daddy will let me. He wants me to stay in and study tomorrow night. But I'll see what I can do. You call me."

"All right," I said, "but first there's something you have to tell me." I turned to her. "Now, please don't think that I'm a jerk, but it wasn't my fault. When Petey introduced us, I didn't——"

At this point I ran into the rear end of a bus. There followed a period of unpleasantness with the bus driver, during which I got a pithy lecture on traffic regulations. I don't know what he had to be sore about. His bus wasn't even nicked. The radiator grille of my car, on the other hand, was a total loss.

And when I got back in the car, there was more grief. The sudden stop had thrown the girl against the windshield head first, and her hat, a little straw number with birds, bees, flowers, and a patch of real grass, was now a heap of rubble. She howled all the way home.

"I'm afraid this evening hasn't been much fun," I said truly as I walked her to her door.

"I'm sorry, Dobie," she sniffled. "I'm sorry all this had to happen to you. You've been so nice to me."

"Oh, it's nothing any young American wouldn't have done," I said.

"You've been very sweet," she repeated. "I hope we'll get to be very good friends."

"Oh, we will. We certainly will."

She was putting her key in the lock.

"Just one more thing," I said. "Before you go in, I have to know——"

"Of course," she said. "I asked you to call and didn't give you my number. It's Kenwood 6817."

"No," I said, "it's not that. I mean yes, I wanted that too. But there's another thing."

"Certainly, Dobie," she whispered and kissed me quickly. Then the door was closed behind her.

"Nuts," I mumbled, got into the car, returned it to the Driv-Ur-Self service, where I left a month's allowance to pay for the broken grille, and went back to the fraternity house.

A few of the guys were sitting in the living room. "Hi, Dobie," called one. "How'd you come out with that smooth operator? Petey sure picked the right night to run off and join the Navy, eh?"

"Oh, she was fine," I answered. "Say, do any of you fellows know her name?"

"No, you lucky dog. She's all yours. Petey just met her this week and you're the only one he introduced her to. No competition. You lucky dog."

"Yeah, sure," I said. "Lucky dog." And I went upstairs to bed.

It was a troubled night, but I had a headful of plans when I got up in the morning. After all, the problem wasn't so difficult. Finding out a girl's name should be no task for a college freshman, a crossword-puzzle expert, and the senior-class poet of the Salmon P. Chase High School, Blue Earth, Minnesota.

First I picked up the phone and dialed the operator. "Hello," I said, "I'd like to find out the name of the people who live at 2123 Fremont Avenue. The number is Kenwood 6817."

"I'm sorry. We're not allowed to give out that information."

I hung up. Then I tried plan No. 2. I dialed Kenwood 6817. A gruff male voice answered, "Hello."

"Hello," I said, "Who is this?"

"Who is *this?*" he said.

"This is Dobie Gillis. Who is this?"

"Who did you wish to speak to?"

Clearly, I was getting nowhere. I hung up.

Then I went and knocked on the door of Ed Beasley's room. Ed was a new pledge of the fraternity, and he was part of my third plan. He opened the door. "Enter, master," he said in the manner required of new pledges.

"Varlet," I said, "I have a task for you. Take yon telephone book and look through it until you find the name of the people who have telephone number Kenwood 6817."

"But, master——" protested Ed.

"I have spoken," I said sharply and walked off briskly, rubbing my palms.

In ten minutes Ed was in my room with Roger Goodhue, the president of the fraternity. "Dobie," said Roger, "you are acquainted with the university policy regarding the hazing of pledges."

"Hazing?"

"You know very well that hazing was outlawed this year by the Dean of Student Affairs. And yet you go right ahead and haze poor Ed. Do you think more of your own amusement than the good of the fraternity? Do you know that if Ed had gone to the dean intead of me we would have had our charter taken away? I am going to insist on an apology right here and now."

Ed got his apology and walked off briskly, rubbing his palms.

"We'll have no more of that," said Roger, and he left too.

I took the phone book myself and spent four blinding hours looking for Kenwood 6817. Then I remembered that Petey had said the girl was new around here. The phone book was six months old; obviously her number would not be listed until a new edition was out.

The only course left to me was to try calling the number again in the hope that she would answer the phone herself. This time I was lucky. It was her voice.

"Hello," I cried, "who is this?"

"Why, it's Dobie Gillis," she said. "Daddy said you called before. Why didn't you ask to talk to me?"

"We were cut off," I said.

"About tonight: I can go to the broadcast with you. I told Daddy we were going to the library to study. So be sure you tell the same story when you get here. I better hang up now. I hear Daddy coming downstairs. See you at eight. 'Bye."

"Goodbye," I said.

And goodbye to some lovely ideas. But I was far from licked. When I drove up to her house at eight in a car I had borrowed from a fraternity brother (I wisely decided not to try the Driv-Ur-Self people again), I still had a few aces up my sleeve. It was now a matter of pride with me. I thought of the day I had recited the senior-class poem at Salmon P. Chase High School and I said to myself, "By George, a man who could do that can find a simple girl's name, by George." And I wasn't going to be stupid about it either. I wasn't going to just ask her. After all this trouble, I was going to be sly about it. Sly, see?

I walked up to the porch, looking carefully for some marker with the family name on it. There was nothing. Even on the mailbox there was no name.

But in the mailbox was a letter! Quickly I scooped it out of the box, just in time to be confronted by a large, hostile man framed in a suddenly open doorway.

"And what, pray, are you doing in our mailbox?" he asked with dangerous calmness.

"I'm Dobie Gillis," I squeaked. "I'm here to call on your daughter. I just saw the mail in the box and thought I'd bring it in to you." I gave him a greenish smile.

"So you're the one who hung up on me this afternoon." He placed a very firm hand on my shoulder. "Come inside, please, young man," he said.

The girl was sitting in the living room. "Do you know this fellow?" asked her father.

"Of course, Daddy. That's Dobie Gillis, the boy who is going to take me over to the library to study tonight. Dobie, this is my father."

"How do you do, Mr. Zzzzzm," I mumbled.

"What?" he said.

"Well, we better run along," I said, taking the girl's hand.

"Just a moment, young man. I'd like to ask you a few things," said her father.

"Can't wait," I chirped. "Every minute counts. Stitch in time saves nine. Starve a cold and stuff a fever. Spare the rod and spoil the child." Meanwhile I was pulling the girl closer and closer to the door. "A penny saved is a penny earned," I said and got her out on the porch.

"It's such a nice night," I cried. "Let's run to the car." I had her in the car and the car in low and picking up speed fast before she could say a word.

"Dobie, you've been acting awfully strange tonight," she said with perfect justification. "I think I want to go home."

"Oh no, no, no. Not that. I'm just excited about our first real date, that's all."

"Sometimes you're so strange, and then sometimes you're so sweet. I can't figure you out."

"I'm a complex type," I admitted. And then I went to work. "How do you spell your name?" I asked.

"Just the way it sounds. What did you think?"

"Oh, I thought so. I just was wondering." I rang up a "No Sale" and started again. "Names are my hobby," I confessed. "Just before I came to get you tonight I was looking through a dictionary of names. Do you know, for instance, that Dorothy means 'gift of God'?"

"No. Really?"

"Yes. And Beatrice means 'making happy,' and Gertrude means 'spear maiden.' "

"Wonderful. Do you know any more?"

"Thousands," I said. "Abigail means 'my father's joy,' Margaret means 'a pearl,' Phyllis means 'a green bough,' and Beulah means 'she who is to be married.' " My eyes narrowed craftily; I was about to spring the trap. "Do you know what your name means?"

"Sure," she said. "It doesn't mean anything. I looked it up once, and it just said that it was from the Hebrew and didn't mean anything."

We were in front of the broadcasting studio. "Curses," I cursed and parked the car.

We went inside and were given tickets to hold. In a moment Dr. Askit took the stage and the broadcast began. "Everyone who came in here tonight was given a ticket," said Dr. Askit. "Each ticket has a number. I will now draw numbers out of this fishbowl here and call them off. If your number is called, please come up on the stage and be a contestant." He reached into the fishbowl. "The first number is 174. Will the person holding 174 please come up here?"

"That's you," said the girl excitedly.

I thought fast. If I went up on the stage, I had a chance to win $64. Not a very good chance, because I'm not very bright about these things. But if I gave the girl my ticket and had her go up. Dr. Askit would make her give him her name and I would know what it was and all this nonsense would be over. It was the answer to my problem. "You go," I told her. "Take my ticket and go."

"But, Dobie——"

"Go ahead." I pushed her out in the aisle.

"And here comes a charming young lady," said Dr. Askit. He helped her to the microphone. "A very lucky young lady, I might add. Miss, do you know what you are?"

"What?"

"You are the ten thousandth contestant that has appeared on the Dr. Askit quiz program. And do you know what I am going to do in honor of this occasion?"

"What?"

"I am going to pay you *ten* times as much as I ordinarily pay contestants. Instead of a $64 maximum, you have a chance to win $640!"

"I may have to pay $640 to learn this girl's name," I thought, and waves of blackness passed before my eyes.

"Now," said Dr. Askit, "what would you like to talk about? Here is a list of subjects."

Without hesitation she said, "Number Six. The meaning of names of girls."

I tore two handfuls of upholstery from my seat.

"The first one is Dorothy," said Dr. Askit.

"Gift of God," replied the girl.

"Right! You now have $10. Would you like to try for $20? All right? The next one is Beatrice."

Two real tears ran down my cheeks. The woman sitting next to me moved over one seat.

"Making happy," said the girl.

"Absolutely correct!" crowed Dr. Askit. "Now would you care to try for $40?"

"You'll be sorry!" sang someone.

"Like hell she will!" I hollered.

"I'll try," she said.

"Gertrude," said Dr. Askit.

"Forty dollars," I mourned silently. A sports coat. A good rod and reel. A new radiator grille for a Driv-Ur-Self car.

"Spear maiden," said the girl.

"Wonderful! There's no stopping this young lady tonight. How about the $80 question? Yes? All right. Abigail. Think now. This is a toughie."

"Oh, that's easy. My father's joy."

"Easy, she said. Easy. Go ahead," I wept, as I pommeled the arm of my seat, "rub it in. Easy!"

"You certainly know your names," said Dr. Askit admiringly. "What do you say to the $160 question? All right? Margaret."

"A pearl."

The usher came over to my seat and asked if anything

was wrong. I shook my head mutely. "Are you sure?" he said. I nodded. He left, but kept looking at me.

"In all my years in radio," said Dr. Askit, "I have never known such a contestant. The next question, my dear, is for $320. Will you try?"

"Shoot," she said gaily.

"Phyllis."

"A green bough."

"Right! Correct! Absolutely correct!"

Two ushers were beside me now. "I see them epileptics before," one whispered to the other. "We better get him out of here."

"Go away," I croaked, flecking everyone near me with light foam.

"Now," said Dr. Askit, "will you take the big chance? The $640 question?"

She gulped and nodded.

"For $640—Beulah."

"She who is to be married," she said.

The ushers were tugging at my sleeves.

"And the lady wins $640! Congratulations! And now, may I ask you your name?"

"Come quietly, bud," said the ushers to me. "Please don't make us use no force."

"Great balls of fire, don't make me go now!" I cried. "Not now! I paid $640 to hear this."

"My name," she said, "is Mary Brown."

"You were sweet," she said to me as we drove home, "to let me go up there tonight instead of you."

"Think nothing of it, Mary Brown," I said bitterly.

She threw back her head and laughed. "You're so funny, Dobie. I think I like you more than any boy I've ever met."

"Well, that's something to be thankful for, Mary Brown," I replied.

She laughed some more. Then she leaned over and kissed my cheek. "Oh, Dobie, you're marvelous."

So Mary Brown kissed me and thought I was marvelous. Well, that was just dandy.

"Marvelous," she repeated and kissed me again.

"Thank you, Mary Brown," I said.

No use being bitter about it. After all, $640 wasn't all the money in the world. Not quite, anyhow. I had Mary Brown, now. Maybe I could learn to love her after a while. She looked easy enough to love. Maybe someday we would get married. Maybe there would even be a dowry. A large dowry. About $640.

I felt a little better. But just a little.

I parked in front of her house. "I'll never forget this evening as long as I live," she said as we walked to the porch.

"Nor I, Mary Brown," I said truthfully.

She giggled. She put her key in the front door. "Would you like to come in, Dobie—dear?"

"No, thanks, Mary Brown. I have a feeling your father doesn't care for me." Then it dawned on me. "Look!" I cried. "Your father. You told him you were at the library tonight. What if he was listening to the radio tonight and heard you on the Dr. Askit program?"

"Oh, don't worry. People's voices sound different over the radio."

"But the name! You gave your name!"

She looked at me curiously. "Are you kiddin'? You know very well I didn't give my right name. . . . DOBIE! WHY ARE YOU BEATING YOUR HEAD AGAINST THE WALL?"

The Mock
Governor

I first saw her in Professor Pomfiritt's political science class. In a sweater. When the class was over, I came up to her. "I'll get right to the point," I said. "I love you."

"You kill me," she said.

"You are the most beautiful woman in the freshman class," I said.

"You knock me out," she said.

"Possibly in the whole University of Minnesota," I said.

"You fracture me," she said.

"Take me to meet your folks," I said.

"They're on a world cruise," she said. "I'm living with my uncle."

"Take me to meet him."

"He won't like you."

"He'll like me."

"You don't know my uncle."

"I know this: he must be beautiful to have such a beautiful niece."

"You got rocks in your head," she said.

"I got a convertible too."

"A convertible head?"

"No, a convertible coupé. Let's go."

We went. We parked down by the riverbank and necked for a couple of hours. Then she said, "My name is Pearl McBride."

"How do you do," I said. "I'm Dobie Gillis."

"How do you do," she said. "What time is it?"

"A quarter to seven."

"Holy smoke, I'm late for dinner. Get me home quick, Dobie. The last time a boy brought me home late my uncle tore off a garage door and broke it over his head."

"Listen," I said, speeding away, "when I get in front of your house, I'll slow down and you jump off."

"Nonsense. You're coming in and meet my uncle."

"But," I trembled, "a garage door——"

"Unless," she said, "you endear yourself to my uncle, our romance will never blossom. You don't want that, do you?"

I looked at her curly blond hair, at her big blue eyes, at her rose-red lips, at her sweater. "No," I said truthfully.

"Then you'll have to face my uncle. He's really not so tough. He's a pushover for flattery. Give him some sweet talk."

"About what?" I asked.

"He's in the construction business. Talk about that."

"I don't know anything about construction."

"You've watched excavations, haven't you?"

"No," I said. "I get dizzy."

"Talk politics to him," Pearl suggested. "He's got an idea that he wants to be governor of Minnesota."

"A commendable ambition. What are his qualifications?"

"A strong handshake," she said.

"Anything else?"

"He smokes cigars and he talks real loud."

"Clearly the man for the job," I said.

"He's been sending up trial balloons, letting it be known around town that he's available for the nomination."

"What's happened?" I asked.

"Silence, mostly. Occasionally some giggles."

We pulled up in front of her house, a six-story concrete bunker with stained-glass windows. "My uncle had some cement left over from a dam he built," she explained.

"How about the windows?"

"Left over from a church. Come on."

"Wait, Pearl," I said, clutching the steering wheel, "perhaps it would be better if I came back tomorrow."

"Come on." She pulled me up the path by my necktie. "Don't forget—flatter him."

The front door opened and out came a livid man about eight feet tall. "Where have you been?" he thundered.

"This is Dobie Gillis," said Pearl. "My uncle, Emmett McBride."

I extended a panicky hand. "I am proud, sir," I squeaked, "to meet the next governor of our state."

For a moment he stared at me. Then his hard red face relaxed. He gave my hand a cartilage-mashing shake. "Come in," he rumbled, "come in."

"You're doing fine," Pearl whispered as we entered.

"Pearl," said McBride, "why haven't you had Dobie over here before?"

"We just met this afternoon," said Pearl, "in a political science class. Dobie is majoring in political science. He thinks politics is the highest pursuit of man, don't you, Dobie?"

"Except maybe construction," I replied.

Pearl beamed. McBride beamed. I beamed. We beamed all three.

"Sit down, Dobie," McBride invited. "Do you smoke cigars?"

"No, sir," I said, "but I admire a man who does."

He lit a Perfecto the size of my forearm. "Now what's all this talk about my being governor?"

"It's all over town, sir."

"Really?"

I prodded him playfully in the ribs. "Now don't pretend," I said with a smile, "that you haven't heard about it."

He chuckled, causing the dinner plates in the next room to rattle. "Well," he admitted, "I know that some of my many friends have been talking about it, but I haven't given them any encouragement."

A note of alarm came into my voice. "Sir, you *will* accept the nomination, won't you?"

"Well, I don't know," he said, dropping a mound of ashes on his vest.

I seized one of his thumbs with my two hands. "But you have to!"

"I don't know. I'm a very busy man, you know."

"You have to," I cried. "It's your duty to the people. Today, as never before, the people need leadership. You cannot shirk the responsibility. Say, you'll accept, Mr. McBride. Say you will."

"Yes," he said simply.

"Perhaps," said Pearl, twinkling, "Dobie will stay for dinner."

"Of course he will," McBride declared. "Pearl, go tell Cook to set an extra place."

Pearl danced merrily into the kitchen.

"I'd offer you a drink," said McBride, "but I don't keep liquor in the house."

"Oh, that's all right," I said, noticing six bottles of bourbon through the half-open door of a cabinet.

"Man in public life has to be careful, you know," he said.

"Of course."

"Not that I miss it," he continued. "I live a very simple life—plain, wholesome food, a good book in the evening, fishing in the summer in our glorious lakes, hunting in the fall in our glorious woods——"

"What do you hunt?" I asked.

"Glorious deer," replied McBride.

"That must be fun," I said. "All I've ever shot are glorious pheasants."

"Ah," he said passionately, "this state abounds with glorious game."

"It's got people too," I said.

"Glorious people," he said.

"Who deserve a glorious governor," I said.

"Dobie," he said.

"Mr. McBride," I said.

"Dinner," Pearl said.

We sat down to a plain wholesome meal of vichyssoise, lobster Newburgh, artichoke hearts, sirloin Chateaubriand, button mushrooms, and peach melba.

After this snack I asked McBride whether I could take Pearl out for a little while.

"Of course, son," he belched, "but be careful with my little girl." He rose laboriously from his chair and put a Neanderthal paw on her shoulder. "My little girl," he bellowed tenderly. "I like to think of Pearl as my own daughter. I've never had any children of my own." He sighed mightily. "Oh, I can't complain. Life's been good to me. But I think I'd trade all this"—his arm swept around the room, indicating a quarter of a million dollars' worth of overstuffed furniture—"for a child of my own. But that's life, I guess." He blew his big red nose.

"Tough," I said.

"Dobie," he said, "I want you to be the first to have one of these." From his breast pocket he removed a McBRIDE FOR GOVERNOR sticker. "Paste it on your windshield."

"How can I thank you enough?" I said.

"Don't try. Run along now and be sure to have Pearl home by ten. Or else," he chuckled, "I will drive you into the ground like a wicket."

I saw him lumbering toward the bourbon as we left. In the car Pearl said, "Now, that wasn't so hard, was it?"

"No," I answered, "but just the same, I'm going to get you home by ten. No sense crowding our luck."

"All right, dear. What shall we do?"

"How about a movie? There's supposed to be a very unusual picture at the Bijou. It *isn't* told in flashback."

"It isn't?" said Pearl. "Then how is it told?"

"They just start at the beginning of the story and go right straight through to the end."

"Revolutionary," said Pearl.

I headed the car toward the Bijou. "Tomorrow night," I suggested, "let's go canoeing."

"Marvy," said Pearl.

"And Friday night we'll go dancing."

"Terrif," said Pearl.

I took her hand. She smiled. I smiled back. Our eyes met. The car ran up on the sidewalk and into a barbershop.

At 11:35 that evening Pearl and I limped up the walk to her house. She had a few yards of tape on her hand. I was uninjured except for a couple of civil and criminal actions pending against me.

McBride came bounding out the door like a big fat jack-in-the-box. "What happened?" he roared.

"Flatter him," Pearl whispered to me and ducked prudently into the house.

"What happened?" repeated McBride, grabbing a handful of my shirt and holding me out at arm's length.

"Oh, sir," I cried, "I can hardly wait until you're governor. The roads in this state are deplorable."

"What," he gritted, "happened?"

"What we need," I said, "is a governor who is also an expert in construction. That's what we need."

He put me down slowly. "What happened?" he asked again.

"You should have seen that disgraceful hole right in the middle of the street," I said. "We'd have both been killed if I hadn't had the presence of mind to drive into a nearby barbershop. Oh, how I wish it was next fall and you were in office."

He rubbed his head for a minute. "How's Pearl?" he asked at length.

"Just a scratch, thank heaven. But there's no telling what will happen to our citizens on these treacherous roads until you are elected and straighten things out."

He sat down on the stoop. "Dobie, listen. You got to be more careful with Pearl. If anything like this ever happens again, I'll——"

"Yes, sir," I interrupted quickly. "I'll be very careful. Good night."

"Good night," he mumbled.

The next night in the canoe, the water lapping softly on the gunwales, the moon bright on Pearl's bandages, she said, "You are a genius."

"Pshaw," I said.

"What a great talent you have for handling people."

"I've got another talent too," I said.

"What?"

"I can tell time. Pearl, it's 9:35. I've got to paddle back to the boat dock and then drive you home by ten. I don't think your uncle Emmett can be pushed much further."

"We'll go in a minute, Dobie. Now lean back."

"Pearl, I think we better leave now."

"Just a few seconds more."

"No."

"Aw, Dobie."

"Well, just a few seconds."

In just a few seconds it was 9:50 and I was frantic. "We'll never make it," I wailed.

"Don't be silly," she said. "It will take you three minutes to get to the boat dock and seven minutes to drive me home. We'll make it."

"Three minutes to the boat dock? You're off your trolley. It took me fifteen minutes to paddle out here."

"Of course," she said. "You were sitting down. Can't make any time that way. Stand up and paddle."

"Stand up?" I asked, aghast.

"Sure. Come on, get up."

"But you're not supposed to stand up in a boat."

"A myth," she said lightly. "Indians did it all the time."

I got up shakily. "I'll tip over the boat," I said.

"Nonsense," said Pearl as I tipped over the boat.

It was a little after midnight when I brought Pearl home in a blanket. "Good luck," she sneezed and ran past Uncle Emmett into the house.

"It's shocking," I yelled as McBride chased me around

the lawn, "the things that go on in this state. Do you know," I asked, vaulting an iron deer, "that there are boats for rent that are not seaworthy? Things," I said, flattening a tulip bed, "have gotten out of hand. What we need in this state is a strong man in the governor's mansion. A man subject neither," I said, capsizing a deck chair, "to fear nor favoritism; a man who will stamp out corruption in high and low places; a man"—he was getting pretty winded—"who will protect the weal of the people; a man stern but just; in short"—he sat abruptly on the grass—"a man like you."

"Dobie," he gasped, "now what have you done?"

"An accident," I replied. "The kind of accident that will not be allowed to happen in your administration."

"Dobie, I'm a patient man——"

"An admirable quality in a governor."

"But this is positively the last time that——"

"Yes, sir. It will never happen again."

"If it does, I'll——"

"Well, I'd better get home now and do some studying for that fascinating political science course. We're having a fascinating test tomorrow. Good night."

He didn't answer.

The next night at the dance I was firm. "We are leaving," I told Pearl, "at nine-thirty."

"But," she protested, "it only takes ten minutes to drive home."

I shook my head and repeated, "We are leaving at nine-thirty."

And promptly at nine-thirty we left. I drove carefully away from the curb. I signaled for all turns, stopped for all lights, passed no cars, kept both hands on the wheel, and never let the speedometer needle get above 25. But all these precautions notwithstanding, halfway home tragedy struck. The motor coughed and died.

I displayed admirable calm. "Pearl," I said quietly, "let us keep our heads. It is twenty minutes before ten. We are a mile from your house. We will get out of the car and walk."

"In these shoes?" asked Pearl, pointing at a pair of flimsy gold things with an arch like a ski slide.

"You can take them off and go barefoot. Or, if you prefer, I'll carry you. In either case, we are leaving immediately. Come on."

"Aren't you even going to lift up the hood and look at the motor?" she asked. "Everybody always does that before they abandon a car."

"I don't know any more about motors than I do about the Koran," I said. "Let's go."

She got out of the car. "Come on, Dobie, let's take a look at the motor. Maybe we'll see something loose or something. Come on, Dobie. It will only take a second to look."

"Oh, all right," I surrendered.

"Goody," she said. "I love to look at motors."

I opened the hood and we peered inside. "You have a nice motor, Dobie," she said.

"Thanks," I murmured.

"All those wires and bolts and things."

"All right, Pearl. We'll start walking now."

"Just a minute, Dobie. I think I see something loose."

"Never mind, Pearl. Let's get going."

"No, Dobie. Look at this little thing over by that little thing."

I looked at this little thing over by that little thing, and sure enough it did seem to have come loose. I fastened it with a pin that seemed to be made for that purpose.

"Now start the car, Dobie. I'll watch."

After extracting a promise from Pearl that we'd leave instantly on foot if the car failed to start, I got back behind the wheel. I stepped on the starter, remembering just too late that the tip of her long, frilly sleeve was resting on the fan belt. There was a ripping and tearing and a pinwheel of flying taffeta.

"It started! It started!" she cried, standing in the street in her dance set.

Uncle Emmett was nowhere in sight when I escorted Pearl up the path, she rakishly dressed in a seat cover.

She slipped into the house. I started tiptoeing back to the car. Then I saw him. Or, rather, I saw a garage door racing toward me like an express train. I executed a twenty-foot standing broad jump, landed on all fours, left the knees of my rented tux on the sidewalk, leaped into the car, and set a world's record for speed in first gear.

For the next several days no moon shone on our romance. We saw one another only by daylight, and when I took her home, I dropped her off a safe six blocks away. It was very unsatisfactory. To our credit it must be said that we worked hard on plans to win over Uncle Emmett, but the best of these plans—for me to grow a mustache and call on Pearl under an assumed name—was none too good. Things looked black.

Then one day before our political science class, Pearl ran up to me in a state of high excitement. I could almost hear her brain clicking. "I've got an idea," she said.

"It better be good."

"It's perfect. Listen, Dobie, what does Uncle Emmett want most in the world?"

"To hit me with a garage door."

She made an impatient gesture. "I'm serious. What does he want most?"

"To be governor."

"Exactly. And there's nothing he won't do for anybody who can make him governor." She prodded my chest with her forefinger. "Dobie, you are going to do it."

"It's too dirty a trick on the people of Minnesota," I said. "I won't do it."

"I don't mean real governor," she said. "I mean mock governor."

"What's that?" I asked. "Someone who goes around mocking the governor?"

"You don't understand," she began as the bell rang for the start of the political science class.

"Let's cut class," I suggested, "and you tell me all about it."

She said, "No, we've got to go to class. That's part of the plan."

I shrugged and followed her in. For an hour I nodded through Professor Pomfritt's lecture. When the class was over I asked Pearl, "Now what?"

"Now we go up and see Professor Pomfritt."

"What are we going to do with him?"

"First we'll flatter him."

"That," I said, "seems to be the standard approach with you."

I followed Pearl up to the lectern where Professor Pomfritt was gathering up his notes and wondering how he was going to live out the year on his salary.

"Professor Pomfritt," said Pearl, "we want to tell you how much we've been enjoying your lectures. Haven't we, Dobie?"

"Yeah," I said.

"Well, thank you, thank you," crowed the professor, his little old eyes crinkling with pleasure.

"We think you give the most stimulating lectures on campus. Don't we, Dobie?"

"Yeah," I said.

"You should have heard me twenty years ago when my lecture notes were still legible," said the professor.

"Nobody," said Pearl, "can accuse you of being an ivory-tower professor. Political science is a living, breathing subject, and the way you teach it is real and vital. Isn't it, Dobie?"

"Yeah," I said.

"Well," chirped the professor. "Well, well, well. I'd ask you up to my rooms for tea only I don't have any tea. However, if you'd like a cup of warm water——"

"No, thanks," said Pearl. "We got another class."

"Bless me, so do I!" exclaimed Professor Pomfritt and started away. "Come up and chat again."

Pearl grabbed his frayed elbow. "There's one thing, Professor. As you know, a new governor will be elected in Minnesota next fall, and there's been a lot of talk about it among the students."

"So that's what they all talk about while I'm lecturing," mused the professor.

"Your inspirational teaching," said Pearl, taking a deep breath, "has got us all so interested in politics that we can't think of anything else."

"We must talk about this some more," said Professor Pomfritt. "Come over tomorrow afternoon. I will borrow some tea leaves from my Chinese laundryman."

Pearl yanked his elbow, shredding the ancient tweed. "This can't wait," she said urgently. "The talk about the election is getting very heated. I'm afraid the students may come to blows."

"Dear me," said the professor. "What's to be done?"

"If I may make a suggestion," she replied, "why not hold a mock election in class? It will be a good practical exercise in political science and it will pacify the students."

The professor looked doubtful. "I don't know. I've never done anything like this before."

"I'm sure," Pearl continued, "that there will be a lot of publicity for our mock election. This being an election year, the newspapers will certainly send reporters."

"Newspapers?" said the professor, brightening. "Ah, good. The last time I had my name in the newspapers I got a raise. It was in 1927. I fainted at the Lindbergh parade. Malnutrition, the papers said, and the dean was forced to increase my salary."

"Then it's all settled?" asked Pearl.

"Very well. But you'll have to help me organize this function. I know so little about these things."

"Don't you worry," Pearl reassured him. "I'll take care of everything. We'll have the mock election on Friday. Just leave all the details to me. Goodbye, Professor, and we wish we had more teachers like you, don't we, Dobie?"

"Yeah," I said.

We left the professor and went outside. "Now," said Pearl, "let's get busy. I'll go around to the newspapers and see that they send reporters. You start working on your speech."

"My speech?"

"You are going to nominate Uncle Emmett with a great speech, a stirring speech, a magnificent speech."

"About him? That's a good trick."

"You can do it, Dobie."

"I can?" I said uncertainly. "Well, I'll try. Tell me something about him. Maybe he has an attractive side that I haven't noticed. What about his education?"

"He quit school in the fifth grade," said Pearl. "He was eighteen and so big that all the other kids used to laugh at him."

"Hm," I said. "Well, maybe that's not so bad. So he didn't have an education. He went to work, rose from the ranks, rags to riches. That's good stuff—a self-made man."

"No," said Pearl. "His father left him the business."

"Maybe," I suggested, "I could say that he's real strong."

Pearl shook her head.

"I doubt," I said, "that I can get him any votes by telling how much he eats."

Pearl had an idea. "Why don't you say something like this? In times of reconstruction we need a construction man."

"And in times of retrenchment we need a trencherman."

"Wait," said Pearl. "You've given me an angle. Reconstruction and retrenchment. For reconstruction, a construction man. For retrenchment, a businessman. Even if Uncle Emmett did inherit the company, you can show that it was his own business ability that made it pay off. He's made scads of money. I'll dig up some facts and figures. You will cite evidence to prove what he has built and how much he has earned. A construction man for reconstruction. A businessman for retrenchment. Uncle Emmett, you will demonstrate, is both."

"It might work," I allowed.

"It *will* work and Uncle Emmett will read all about your speech in the papers and he will welcome you back like a long lost son and we can start necking at night again."

"What are we waiting for?" I said, rubbing my hands briskly. "Let's get started."

By election time on Friday we were ready. Pearl had alerted the newspapers. I had composed an eloquent speech based on data that Pearl had copied from a ledger she found in her uncle's desk. Our plans were well laid and synchronized. We were confident.

Pearl, the self-appointed chairwoman, stepped to the lectern. At a table on the side of the room sat a dozen reporters, about whom Professor Pomfritt, with new leather patches on his elbows, hovered like a genial bee. The students were in a festive mood. Pearl rapped for silence.

"Nominations," she said, "are now in order."

I stood and was recognized. "Ladies and gentlemen," said I, loud and clear, "I want to tell you about a fellow Minnesotan named Emmett McBride. Emmett McBride is in the construction business. In the last few years Emmett McBride has constructed the following edifices at the following profits: the First National Bank of Minneapolis—$1,583,087; the St. Cloud-Chaska highway—$987,-590; the Rochester reservoir—$798,679; the Sauk Center viaduct—$807,234; the Bemidji causeway—$694,589."

"Hooray!" shouted Pearl from the chair.

"I mention these figures," I said, "to prove two things. First, that Emmett McBride is a construction man, Second, that Emmett McBride is a businessman."

"Hooray!" shouted Pearl from the chair.

"In these parlous days of reconstruction and retrenchment," I went on, "do we want a politician in the governor's mansion?"

"No!" shouted Pearl from the chair.

"Do we want a theorist in the governor's mansion?"

"No!" shouted Pearl from the chair.

"Do we want a visionary in the governor's mansion?"

"No!" shouted Pearl from the chair.

"What do we want in the governor's mansion?" I asked.

"A construction man and a businessman," shouted Pearl from the chair.

"Exactly," I said. "And since we can't have two governors, we must find a man who is both a construction man and a businessman. Emmett McBride is both. In these parlous days of reconstruction and retrenchment, we want Emmett McBride in the governor's mansion, that's who we want."

"Hooray!" shouted Pearl from the chair, and from the students the cry came back, "Hooray!"

"Few of you," I said, "have ever heard of Emmett McBride. He has never been a candidate for office. It is fitting that the discovery of Emmett McBride should be made at this university which has been the scene of so many other great discoveries. Here is the source of progress in this state. The people look to us for leadership. Let us supply that leadership. Let us elect Emmett McBride!"

Before the mounting cheers could get out of control, Pearl shouted, "I move that McBride be elected by acclamation."

"You can't make a motion from the chair," cried some finicky parliamentarian, but his voice was lost as the entire assemblage in full-throated uproar acclaimed Emmett McBride the victor.

Then I was hoisted on several shoulders and carried around the room. "Uncle Emmett will love you," yelled Pearl as I was carried past her.

"How about his niece?" I asked as I circled her the second time and she nodded energetically and blew kisses.

"I'll be over tomorrow morning—after he's had a chance to read the papers," I said the third time around.

It was all on the front pages the next morning, and I drove to Pearl's house whistling all the way. I walked boldly up the path, threw open the door without knocking, and called cheerily, "Where is lovable old Uncle Emmett?"

Pearl, lying prone on the living-room sofa, lifted a tear-stained face. She looked at me for an instant, then scrambled to her feet. "Run for your life," she cried. "Leave the city. Leave the state. Leave the country if possible."

"What's the gag?" I asked, mystified.

"Hurry! Uncle Emmett will be home any minute. He's already raised his bail."

"Bail?"

"You read the papers, Dobie—all those figures you gave about Uncle Emmett's profits."

"So?"

"So they arrested him this morning for income tax evasion."

Boy Bites Man

I am the type citizen who counts his blessings and lets sleeping dogs lie and doesn't look gift horses in the mouth.

Far was it from me to complain because my girl Lola Pfefferkorn had one teensy-weensy shortcoming: she was as dumb as a post. This I could overlook when I considered her obvious advantages. She had hair like spun gold and lips like the red, red rose, and eyes where dwelt enchantment, and a figure that brought forth frequent cries of admiration from my slightly foam-flecked lips. She was rich too; she had inherited real estate all over Minneapolis.

So I would say to myself as Lola and I walked arm in arm across the campus, the object of envious glances, I would say to myself, I'd say, "Brains aren't everything. In Lola's case, hardly anything."

Sometimes, I'll confess, I would become a little irritated at Lola. Like the time she locked her keys inside her car for safekeeping. Or the time she tried to buy a ticket for the football game between Minnesota and Open Date. But my irritation would soon disappear. I would take another look at Lola and I wasn't mad any more.

I first met Lola in a freshman journalism class. What she was doing in a journalism class, or in college for that matter, I won't attempt to answer. My own presence in the journalism class, on the other hand, is easily explained. Ever since I was editor of the yearbook at the Salmon P. Chase high school in Blue Earth, Minnesota, I have known that journalism and I were made for each other. Why, I even look like a reporter. I always wear my hat on the back of my head and chainsmoke cigarettes and carry a big wad of yellow paper in my pocket and shout over the telephone.

Oh, I was a natural for journalism all right, and the University of Minnesota was the natural place for me to study it. Because at the University of Minnesota journalism was not just a matter of reading textbooks and doing homework. Here you got practical experience in addition to academic theory. For two weeks out of every year, students were required to go to work as cub reporters on the downtown Minneapolis newspapers, where they covered real news stories and helped to put out a real metropolitan daily. This type work, as I had so ably demonstrated at the Salmon P. Chase high school in Blue Earth, Minnesota, was all grist for my mill.

But I digress. I was telling about Lola. I first saw her in the freshman journalism class. She was sitting across the room. I smiled at her. She smiled back. I wrote her a note:

"Dear Stacked: Will you have a coke with me after class?"

She nodded.

I borrowed a dime from a rich kid sitting next to me. We had a coke. We talked. I told her all about myself, my early life, my accomplishments, my ambitions. She asked me whether I had heard Tommy Dorsey's new record of "Be There, Ingrid, When the Oats Are Green."

The next day I borrowed a dollar and we had lunch. We talked. I told her about the state of the nation, intrigues in international politics, the need for a favorable balance of world trade. She asked me whether I could do the Samba.

Our romance budded. When I started to do her homework, it bloomed. We were seen everywhere together: dances, shows, sleigh rides, hayrides, wiener roasts, night court. Occasionally we would spend an evening at home just sitting before the fire and having a long conversation —I talking, she dozing.

It was natural that Lola and I should stick together when it came time to go to work for two weeks on a downtown Minneapolis paper. We chose the Minneapolis *Sentinel*, a fine old newspaper and entirely worthy of my talents.

We walked into the city room, stated our business and were directed to see Mr. Oliver, the city editor. Hand in hand, we approached his littered desk. "How do you do, sir," I said. "This is Lola Pfefferkorn and I am Dobie Gillis. We're from the University of Minnesota and we're going to work here for two weeks.

"Perhaps it would help," I continued, "if I told you a little about us. I am what might be called a natural reporter, a born newsman. I think you will find me well qualified to fill any assignment, particularly the reporting of public affairs. May I suggest that you assign me to cover City Hall?

"Now, Miss Pfefferkorn's talents are not so clearly defined. Her abilities, you might say, have not yet crystallized. Perhaps it would be better to just give her a roving assignment. Let her wander about the city and interview people. She is quite familiar with Minneapolis; her father had large real-estate holdings here."

"Let go of her hand," said Mr. Oliver. "Take off your hat. Put out that cigarette. Stop leaning on my desk. Pull up your necktie. Wipe that grin off your face. Stop shuffling your feet. Take your hat off my desk. Close your mouth."

"I want to go home," said Lola.

"This," said Mr. Oliver, "is a city room. This is a place of business. Stop sniffling, little girl. Let me tell you two something. I think college students belong in college. Not in my city room. Unfortunately, my employer doesn't see it my way. He no longer allows me to throw college

students out of here bodily. He says it gives the paper a
bad name. But"—Mr. Oliver picked up a pair of long
shears and waved them ominously—"the very first bit of
nonsense out of either of you and out you go. Both of you.
Is that clear?"

"I want to go home," said Lola.

"Hush, dear," I said. "All city editors have to talk that
way. It's part of their job."

Mr. Oliver growled in his throat. He pointed the shears
at me. "You, wanted City Hall. All right. Your beat will
be the office of the commissioner of public works."

"Come now, Mr. Oliver," I said, chuckling, "nothing
ever happens in the office of the commissioner of public
works."

"Exactly," said Mr. Oliver. "And you, little girl, will
write obituaries. And if you ever come into this office
again wearing knee-length slacks, somebody will be writing your obituary.

"The deadline for the noon edition is 11 A.M. The
deadline for the home edition is 2 P.M. The deadline for
the final edition is three-thirty. Now beat it."

"I'll be back and get you for lunch," I said hurriedly
to Lola and fled to the office of the commissioner of public works in City Hall.

"Come in, come in," boomed Mr. O'Toole, the commissioner of public works, his big red jowls curved in a
smile. "Always happy to receive the press. You're new on
the *Sentinel*, aren't you, son? I haven't seen you before."

"Well, sir," I confessed, "I'm just on the *Sentinel* temporarily. I'm a journalism student at the university and
I'm working on the *Sentinel* for two weeks to get experience."

"Splendid!" said Mr. O'Toole. "That's just fine. Nothing like an education, I always say. My own boys are students at the Ingelbretsvold Manual Training School.
Here's their picture."

I looked at a portrait of two adenoidal hulks. "Fine-
looking boys," I said.

Mr. O'Toole beamed. "Here's a picture of their mother," he said.

A toothy harridan leered out of the frame. "Damn handsome woman," I said.

"Nothing like a family," declared Mr. O'Toole. "Nothing like coming home after a hard day in the service of the people and finding your wife and children waiting for you, ready to soothe your cares and lift your spirits. Then sitting down to a well-cooked meal of simple food and afterward all playing Twenty Questions or bobbing for apples or maybe reading aloud from a volume of Dickens."

Mr. O'Toole pulled out a handkerchief and brushed aside a tear. "Oh, why," he asked, "must people spend their lives in a frenzied chase after money and power when right in their own homes they can find riches more precious than gold?"

"Search me," I said.

"The homely virtues," said Mr. O'Toole, "are the best. Nothing like a home and children and friendship and love and mother and honesty and the Constitution."

"To be sure," I agreed. "Now how about some news."

"Well," said Mr. O'Toole, "we just got a new motor for our snow plow."

"That's real nice," I said, "but don't you have something a little more sensational?"

Mr. O'Toole chuckled. "I'm afraid not, son. Nothing much ever happens in this office."

"Yes," I said sadly.

"I just try to do my job with quiet efficiency and selfless devotion to the needs of the people."

We shook hands silently.

"Aren't you building any roads?" I asked. "Or perhaps a bridge or a culvert or maybe an airport?"

Mr. O'Toole looked at me sharply. "What have you heard about an airport?" he asked.

"Nothing. Nothing at all. I was just wondering."

"Yeah?" he said. "Yeah?" He looked at me for a long

time. Then his eyes narrowed with thought. He rubbed
his chin.

"Son," he said, "how long have you been working on
the *Sentinel?*"

"I just started this morning."

"I see. Have you had any previous newspaper experience?"

"Indeed I have. I was editor of the yearbook at the
Salmon P. Chase high school in Blue Earth, Minnesota."

"Is that so? Tell me, my boy, how much do you know
about the organization of a city government? For example, what do you know about the offices in City Hall?"

"Not much," I confessed. "But I learn real quick."

"Uh huh," said Mr. O'Toole. He drummed on the desk
with his finger tips for a few minutes. Then he looked up
at me and smiled. "Son," he said heartily, "I like to see a
young man get ahead. I'm going to do a fine thing for
you. I'm going to give you a scoop."

"Oh, happy day," I said. "A scoop."

"Do you know," asked Mr. O'Toole, "where Forty
Acres is?"

"Vaguely," I said. "It's somewhere in north Minneapolis, isn't it?"

"Yes. Have you ever been there?"

"No."

"Good," said Mr. O'Toole. "As you may have heard,
there has been a lot of agitation in Minneapolis for a
new airport. The present airport on the south side is too
close to the river bluffs. Pilots have been complaining
that it's too hard to land there, especially at night. So
people have been talking more and more about building
a new airport on the north side. As commissioner of
public works, I am in charge of choosing a site. Now I'll
give you your scoop. The new airport is going to be built
on Forty Acres. I'm signing a contract for the land the
first thing tomorrow morning. I wasn't going to release
the story to the papers until tomorrow, but I've decided
to give you a break."

"What a story!" I cried. "Leave me to a phone!"

"Wait a minute," said Mr. O'Toole, rising and taking a firm grip on my lapels. "I'm giving you this story on one condition."

"What's that?"

"You are not to write this story until the deadline for the final edition of the *Sentinel*. You will not write it for the noon edition and you will not write it for the home edition. You will hold it for the final edition."

"But," I protested, "the final edition doesn't come out until four-thirty this afternoon."

"I know," said Mr. O'Toole. "I want this story in that edition and I don't want it in any earlier edition."

"But why?"

Mr. O'Toole gave me a fatherly pat on the shoulder. "You wouldn't understand," he said. "Now promise me that you won't write it for any edition before the final. If not, I'll have to ask you not to use the story."

I shook my head helplessly.

"Promise me," said Mr. O'Toole.

"All right," I said finally. "I promise."

I left Mr. O'Toole's office puzzled. Why does he want to wait for the final edition? I wondered. Why? I sat down on a bench in the corridor of City Hall to ponder the puzzle. I searched my brain for a single good reason.

Suddenly my reverie was shattered as a man carrying a huge stack of maps tripped and fell over my outstretched legs.

"Oh, I'm sorry," I cried, leaping up.

"It's all right," he said. "I was carrying so many maps I couldn't see where I was going."

"Let me help you pick them up," I offered. I bent down and scooped up an armful of maps.

"Thank you," he said. "Now if you'll just put them on top of this pile——"

"Oh no," I said. "I'll help you carry them. Where do they go?"

"Well, if you don't mind. Right down the hall to the county surveyor's office."

I followed him down the hall and into a room that was crowded with maps of all description. Maps were tacked on the walls, piled on tables, and heaped on the floor.

"Just put them down anywhere," he said.

"Say," I said, "this looks like an interesting place. What are all these maps?"

"These," he explained, "are detail maps of every section of Minneapolis. Look around if you want to. Is there any particular section of the city you are interested in?"

"No," I said. Then I bethought myself. If I was going to write a story about the new airport, it might be a good idea to look at Forty Acres. "Do you have a map of Forty Acres?"

"Sure. Right over here in the north Minneapolis section. Here it is right here. See?"

"Oh yes. Tell me, what does this mark mean?"

"That? That means a swamp. Forty Acres is all marshland. The whole thing is a bog, and there are patches of quicksand all through it. Horrible place."

"Is that so?" I said, bewildered. "It doesn't sound like a good site for an airport, does it?"

"Worst possible site," he answered. "Now, if I wanted to build an airport in north Minneapolis, I'd choose this land right over here next to Forty Acres. It's called Minnehaha Heights. It's perfect for an airport. See here. There's excellent drainage on all sides. It's on a kind of little plateau. Flat as a table on top and forty feet of solid rock underneath. Long enough for runways and wide enough for taxi strips. Perfect."

"Strange," I murmured.

"I'd like to spend some more time with you," he said, "but I go out to lunch now. Would you care to join me? We can come back here afterward."

"Lunch!" I exclaimed, remembering my date with Lola. "Thank you very much, but I've got to run."

All the way back to the *Sentinel* office my brain was clicking like a metronome. Something was very stinky, that was clear. Why was O'Toole buying Forty Acres

when Minnehaha Heights was right next to it? Why did
he want me to hold the story until the final edition?
O'Toole was up to something and it wasn't honest.

I burst into the city room ready to spill my discovery
to Mr. Oliver. But a strange sight greeted my eyes. The
entire cityroom staff was assembled in a half circle
around Mr. Oliver's desk. To one side stood Lola, quaking
in her culottes.

"Ah," cried Mr. Oliver upon seeing me, "just in time.
Sit down, Gillis, and listen to this obituary that your
friend Lola has just written. I want everyone to hear
this."

I sat down.

Mr. Oliver began reading:

" 'No more will the flowers raise their multicolored
heads and smile for Emmett T. Zoldin, upholsterer, of
475 Coolidge Ave. No more will the song of birds cheer
his days. The winds will still blow and the rain will
still fall upon the green earth, but Emmett T. Zoldin will
not know.

" 'For yesterday as Emmett T. Zoldin was bent over a
Swedish Modern chaise longue in his upholstery shop,
the Angel of Death with merciful swiftness extinguished
the flickering candle of his life.

" 'And no amount of tears from Yetta Zoldin, his wid-
ow, or from their son, Sam O. Zoldin, or from their daugh-
ter, Mrs. Arbutus Gottschalk, or from Emmett's brother
Pyotor, still living in their native Finmark, will bring
Emmett T. Zoldin back. And tomorrow when the Abide
With Me Mortuary lays his mortal remains to rest in
Sunnyvale Cemetery, it will be the end of Emmett T.
Zoldin on this earth.

" 'Farewell, honest upholsterer!' "

Mr. Oliver turned to Lola. "Where," he screamed,
"where in the name of all that's good and holy did you
learn to write an obituary like that?"

Lola burst into tears.

"Of all the lousy, crummy, garish, flamboyant, undis-
ciplined, stupid, corny writing," continued Mr. Oliver,

"that I have ever had the misfortune to read, this is absolutely the—— Will you stop blubbering?"

Lola cried louder.

"Please, little girl," begged Mr. Oliver, "please, please stop crying."

Lola shifted into high.

"For heaven's sake, stop!" shrieked Mr. Oliver. "I can't stand to hear a woman cry. Please, please, please. I'm sorry. I'll give you anything you want. Please stop crying!"

"I didn't want to write any old obituaries," wailed Lola. "Why can't I go out and interview people like Dobie said?"

"All right! All right! Just get out of here. Get out of my sight. Go anywhere. Do anything you want to. But get out of here."

Everyone stood up and went to his own desk. Lola came over to me and laid damp eyes on my shoulder. "There, there," I said. I turned to Mr. Oliver. "Sir," I said, "there's something I want to talk to you about."

"You!" he shouted. "Get out! Out! Out! Out! Both of you. Out!"

He grabbed the shears and started after us.

We decided to leave.

Lola and I sat at lunch. "I wonder," she said, "who I should interview. I don't know anybody."

"I don't know," I said. "Listen, Lola, I ran into something big this morning. There's some shady work going on down at City Hall. I saw O'Toole this morning, the commissioner of public works."

"Maybe," interrupted Lola, "I could interview O'Toole."

I made an impatient gesture. "Listen, Lola, I think I'm on the trail of something big." I told her what had happened.

"Oh, listen to the juke box," she said. "That's Guy Lombardo playing 'I'll Never Waltz This Waltz Again, Walter, Unless I Waltz It with You.'"

"I know that O'Toole's a crook. I don't know why he wanted me to hold the story until the final edition, but I know that only a crook would build an airport at Forty Acres when Minnehaha Heights is right next to it. . . . Lola, you're not paying any attention to me."

"I am too. I can listen to you and take off my nail polish at the same time."

"I'm going back to City Hall and find out some things," I said. "And when I get back, you can bet that Mr. Oliver is going to listen to me this time."

"Take me too," said Lola. "I'll go interview O'Toole."

"Can't you think of anybody better to interview than that crook?"

"Now, Dobie, don't you pick on me too."

"Aaah—all right."

I took her down to City Hall and deposited her in O'Toole's office while I went to ask some questions of my friend in the county surveyor's office. I carefully wrote down what he told me. I thanked him and went to the office of the register of deeds.

From there I went to the City Hall reference library and looked up a name in the city directory. Next I went to the city health department for some information. After that I stopped and saw the clerk of probate court. Then I saw the clerk of district court. Then I went to the marriage license bureau. My last stop was the register of births.

It was three o'clock when I finished my rounds. I had all the facts I needed and time enough to write the story for the final edition. I ran out of City Hall and grabbed a cab back to the *Sentinel*. O'Toole, I thought grimly as I rode, is going to get a story in the final edition all right, but it won't be the story he thinks.

I went right to Mr. Oliver's desk. He wasn't going to chase me away this time. "Tear out the front page!" I shouted as I drew up before him. "I've got the story of the year!"

"You whelp," said Mr. Oliver, reaching for his shears. "You call yourself a reporter. I assigned you to cover the commissioner of public works, the easiest beat in town, and you muffed it. If it hadn't been for Lola we wouldn't have had the story. I may have misjudged her, but I was right about you. You stink."

"What story? What are you talking about?" I asked in amazement.

Mr. Oliver shoved a copy of the home edition toward me. "How could you have missed that story? Why, if Lola hadn't stopped in to interview O'Toole, we never would have had it."

I looked at the front page. Waves of disbelief passed over me. No, it couldn't be!

But there it was, headline and all:

NEW MUNICIPAL AIRPORT TO BE
BUILT AT MINNEHAHA HEIGHTS

August R. O'Toole, commissioner of public works, revealed exclusively to the *Sentinel* this afternoon that a new municipal airport will soon be constructed at Minnehaha Heights in north Minneapolis.

"Lola!" I gasped. "Where's Lola? I've got to see Lola."

"She's at her desk," said Mr. Oliver. "Now, Gillis, I've got some things to say to——"

But I didn't stay. I ran across the office to Lola's desk. She was putting up her hair. "Lola!" I yelled.

"Hello, Dobie," she said brightly.

"Lola! Where did you get that story?"

"From Mr. O'Toole."

"Did he say that he was going to build the airport at Minnehaha Heights?"

"Well——"

"Did he?"

"Well, not exactly."

"Then why did you write that story?"

"Well, it's your fault, Dobie."

"*My* fault? In God's name, why?"

"Because you said at lunch today that only a crook would build an airport at Forty Acres when Minnehaha

Heights is right next to it. And I know that Mr. O'Toole is not a crook. Therefore he wouldn't build an airport at Forty Acres. Therefore he's going to build one at Minnehaha Heights. See?"

She went back to fixing her hair.

I sat down. "Now, Lola," I said, "let's go through this once more. Slowly. You say that if Mr. O'Toole is not a crook he won't build the airport at Forty Acres."

"That's what you said."

"All right. That's what I said. And you say that he's going to build the airport at Minnehaha Heights because he's not a crook."

She nodded.

"How," I screamed, "do you know that he's not a crook?"

"Dobie," said Lola, "you've talked to Mr. O'Toole. You've heard him speak of his wife and children, how they bob for apples after dinner and play Twenty Questions. You've heard him say that there is nothing like a home and children and friendship and love and mother and the Constitution.

"How," concluded Lola triumphantly, "could such a man be a crook?"

"Great balls of fire!" I said slowly. "Great balls of fire." I slapped myself in the forehead several times. "And that is why you wrote your story."

"Of course, silly. You got any gum, Dobie?"

I took both her hands and looked deep into her eyes. "Lola, do you know what you have done?" I asked.

But she never got a chance to answer. Because suddenly blazing across the city room in a whirl of paper and overturning typewriters came Mr. Oliver and Mr. O'Toole.

"You!" screamed Mr. Oliver.

"You!" screamed Mr. O'Toole.

Lola leaped on my lap.

"I'll have you thrown in jail," bellowed Mr. O'Toole. "I'll have you run out of town. I'll sue. I'll prosecute. I'll have you tarred and feathered."

"I'll drum you out of the business," roared Mr. Oliver.

"I'll see to it that you never set foot in a newspaper office again. I'll put you on every blacklist in the country."

O'Toole took over. "You Jezebel. You lying, thieving, sneaking shrew. You double-tongued hag. You viper. You deceitful witch."

I am the type guy that can be pushed just so far and no farther. I spilled Lola off my lap and stood up. I pointed a finger at O'Toole.

"You," I snarled. "You are a fine one to call people names. You crook. You thief. You embezzler."

"Now, just a minute——" began O'Toole.

"Just a minute yourself. Sit down, O'Toole. You too, Oliver. You're going to listen to me for a while.

"This afternoon," I said, "I made some very interesting discoveries in the City Hall. First I went to the office of the register of deeds."

O'Toole blanched.

"I looked up the title to Forty Acres," I went on. "It was listed under the name of Abel Hanson. I went to the city directory to find out who Abel Hanson was. His name was not listed. I figured that he might have died, so I went to the health department and looked at their mortality records. Abel Hanson was dead all right."

O'Toole squirmed.

"So," I said, "I went to the clerk of probate court to find out who was the executor of Abel Hanson's estate. I learned that he had died without heirs and without leaving a will. Probate court had appointed the Mill City Trust Corporation as executor.

"That didn't tell me very much, so I went to the clerk of district court to look up the articles of incorporation of the Mill City Trust Corporation. I found that it was owned by four men: John Guthrie, Harold Peters, Arthur Goodkind, and George Gilfillan.

"Playing a hunch, I went to the marriage license bureau. I looked up the marriage license of August R. O'Toole."

O'Toole wiped his brow.

"I found that O'Toole was married on July 8, 1925,

to one Agnes Gilfillan. I went over to the register of births. I found that Agnes Gilfillan and George Gilfillan, curiously enough, were brother and sister.

"Your brother-in-law, O'Toole, is executor of Forty Acres. That's why you were going to buy that swamp for an airport. There was going to be plenty in it for you and your brother-in-law to split.

"And now I know why you wanted me to hold that story for the final edition. You wanted the story to be in the paper before you signed the contract for Forty Acres. You didn't want to be accused of making the transaction secretly. But you didn't want the story to be in an early edition because then there would have been a chance that somebody would have gone to City Hall and looked up all those things that you thought I wasn't smart enough to find out. You knew very well that the offices at City Hall close at four o'clock and that the final edition isn't on the streets until four-thirty. Anybody who saw the story in the paper and wanted to make an investigation wouldn't be able to start until tomorrow morning. And you were going to sign the contract first thing in the morning."

Mr. Oliver was on his feet now. He came over and put his arm around me. "What do you say, O'Toole?" he asked.

O'Toole swallowed several times. "Why, the whole thing is preposterous," he said. "Absolutely ridiculous. I don't know what this boy is talking about. I never had the slightest intention of buying Forty Acres. I was going to buy Minnehaha Heights all the time. Why, it says so in the paper."

"Scram, O'Toole," said Mr. Oliver. "Get out. And don't let me see your name on the ticket at election time this fall. Do you understand?"

"Eh?" said O'Toole. "What? What's that? Oh yes. Yes, of course. I—I was thinking of retiring anyhow. Twelve years of quiet devotion to the service of the people, a man needs a rest. Yes."

"Out," said Mr. Oliver.

O'Toole left. Fast.

"Dobie," said Mr. Oliver with strange tenderness, "I don't know what to say. As long as I'm alive, you can have a job on this paper. And as for you, young lady, if I never see——"

"Lay off her, Mr. Oliver," I said. "She's a good kid."

Mr. Oliver paused, shook his head sadly, and went back to his desk.

"Lola," I said, "let's face it. You're just not bright."

"I guess you're right, Dobie."

"I got you off this time, Lola, but frankly, I'm worried about you. I may not always be around to save you. You've got to learn to think for yourself, Lola. You've got to discipline your mind. All you ever think about is dancing and tobogganing. There are more important things in life, Lola.

"Sometimes, Lola, I wish that you were poor. Then you would have to think about making a living. Then you would have to consider the hard, practical things of life. But, of course, you never give a thought to money."

"I wonder how much the city will pay for Minnehaha Heights," said Lola, piling up her back hair.

"Life is real, Lola, life is earnest and—— What's that? How much will the city pay for Minnehaha Heights? Quite a bit, I'm sure. Why do you ask?"

"Because," said Lola, pulling a wisp of hair off her shell-like ear, "I own it."

The King's English

I used to have a convertible with long, rakish lines and a girl named Poppy Herring, also with long, rakish lines. It was Poppy's lines—and only her lines—that won my heart. The attraction was entirely physical. Mentally, emotionally, spiritually, we were light-years apart. I am sensitive, she was crass. I am romantic; she was commercial. I am a flute; she was a trumpet. I am old ivory; she was stainless steel.

But being a worshiper of beauty, I could not resist her. She had so much beauty to worship that I almost had to put on an extra man. Her symmetry, the architecture of her limbs, the melody of her movements, her planes and hollows, her peaks and valleys—all this was more than I could withstand. I was mad for her the moment I saw her.

Our first meeting occurred in Professor Snaith's freshman English class on the opening day of the spring semester. I had gotten to class a little early and was already seated when Poppy came in. She took the chair next to mine. She was dressed in a dirndl and a peasant blouse that revealed one creamy shoulder. I turned to her with a smile of frank admiration. She looked at me with some nervousness and hitched up the blouse to cover the exposed shoulder. At this, the other shoulder came uncovered. My smile broadened. She seized the blouse with two hands and pulled it up over both her shoulders. This proved unsatisfactory—to her, not to me—because now the neckline of the blouse popped out in a sort of massive *décolletage*. I clapped my hands delightedly.

"How would you like a hit in the eye?" she inquired in a hostile manner.

I was preparing a soft answer when Professor Snaith walked into the classroom. "I'll talk to you later," I whispered and turned my attention to the professor. Physically, he was not an imposing man. He was little and bent. Only a few white hairs remained on his lumpy cranium. His eyes were beady, his nose was overlong, his thin lips curved downward in a perpetual sneer. His ancient blue serge suit gleamed dully, like the sides of a hearse.

Unprepossessing though he was, I still looked at him with respect. For Professor Snaith was a renowned scholar. His book, *Snaith's English Usage,* was the standard freshman text in hundreds of American colleges. On matters concerning grammar and diction, he had been a universally accepted authority for more than thirty years.

Not to brag, but I was a bit of an authority on English usage myself. Having literary ambitions, I was naturally concerned with the English language. I had devoted years to a careful study of the mother tongue; I doubt whether there was another eighteen-year-old man in the country with such a command of the language as I. But immense as my knowledge of the subject was, I still felt that I might learn something from an expert like Professor Snaith. Indeed, the reason I had come to the University of Minnesota in the first place was because Professor Snaith taught there.

The professor rapped on the lectern for attention. When the class was quiet, he began. "Owing to the fact that this is the first day of the semester," he said, "I shall dismiss the class early. . . . You will note that I said *owing to* and not *due to. Due to* is incorrect unless preceded by the verb *to be.* For instance, you may say, 'The postponement of the ball game was due to rain.' But you may not say, 'Due to rain the ball game was postponed.' "

I raised my hand.

"Yes?" said the professor impatiently.

I rose and addressed him with a friendly smile. "Sir," I said, "I am not unmindful of your eminence as an English scholar. Believe me, I intend no disrespect when I tell you that you are wrong."

"Wrong, did you say?" he asked, looking at me incredulously.

I nodded ruefully. "Yes, sir. You say *due to* must be preceded by the verb *to be*. But I use it without the verb *to be*. So does my whole family. So do all my friends. So do all the people I've ever talked to or listened to. Yet you say it is incorrect. Wake up, my dear man. Can everyone be out of step but you?"

His jaw dropped open.

"Language," I continued, warming to my favorite subject, "is a living, growing, changing thing. And what makes it live, grow, change? The people, of course. Language belongs to the people, and the way they use it is the correct way. Correctness is determined not by antiquated rules but by public usage. Anyone who takes another view is doctrinaire, reactionary, and obsolete. Thank you." I sat down.

The professor had turned a curious blackish color. Only the area around his lips remained white, which gave him somewhat the appearance of a desiccated minstrel man. For several minutes he seemed to be unable to speak, but finally he found his tongue.

"In the forty years I have devoted to this underpaid profession of teaching," he said in heated tones, "I have heard many an asinine outburst, but never one so asinine as yours. I can only assume that your mind has been unhinged by your recent passage through puberty.

"Do you realize," he said, his voice mounting to a roar, "that centuries of scholarship and the efforts of countless brilliant minds have gone into the codification of the English language? You presumptuous driveler, how dare you suggest that the rules of English usage must give way to the ungrammaticisms of factory hands, hostlers, and college freshmen? You cretinous barbarian, would you exchange the elegance of Macaulay and Addison for the thick-tongued mouthings of every underbred Tom, Dick, and Harry? The rules of usage have been established. In this class they shall be enforced. The tide of vulgarization shall not spill over my threshold. And in future, you will please keep your oafish opinions to yourself."

"But, sir——" I cried, blushing hotly.

He silenced me with a withering glare and addressed the entire class. "That is all for today. The textbook used in this course is *Snaith's English Usage.* You will find it at any campus bookstore. See that you are all supplied with copies when the class meets tomorrow. Class dismissed."

I was blazing with indignation as I left the classroom. Here I had just tried to enlighten a man, and what did I get in return? Insults and vilification, that's what. The mossbacked old fool! Bumbling along with his pack of obsolete dogma, turning like an adder on anyone who represented progress and truth. Well, I'd get even some day. Someday he'd be good and sorry.

As I came into the corridor I caught a glimpse of Poppy, walking out of the building. A surge of longing overwhelmed me, erasing the memory of my recent humiliation at the hands of Professor Snaith. I raced outdoors after Poppy and grasped her arm. "Hello," I said with a winsome smile.

"Let go of my arm," she replied. "The last wolf that made a pass at me is now eating through a tube."

"But you misunderstand," I protested. "I have no designs on you. My admiration is of the highest order."

She gave a doubting snort.

"No, truly," I insisted. "I am a worshiper of beauty, a terribly sensitive fellow. You appeal to me aesthetically. I am thinking of writing a poem about you."

"You write poetry?" she asked, giving me a hard look.

"A little," I confessed with lowered eyelids. "Of course it's not very good, but someday I hope to be a fine poet."

She shook her head decisively. "From this you won't make a living," she declared.

I shrugged. "There are more important things."

"Like what?"

"Truth, beauty, art——"

"Goodbye, friend," said Poppy. "I'll see you around." She started away.

I clung. "What's wrong?" I cried.

"Listen, whatever your name is——"

"Dobie Gillis."

"Listen, Dobie Gillis, I've got three sisters, all married, all with kids. Since 1945 all three of my sisters combined have had a total of two new dresses. Why? Because they all married rabbits."

"How very odd!" I exclaimed. "Real rabbits?"

"No, stupid. I mean they married guys with no drive, no gumption. Very cultured types, all of them. One plays a fiddle, one paints water colors, one models in clay. Truth, beauty, art—they're crawling with it. But not one of them makes a living."

"Ah," I said. "So you are afraid of becoming involved with an artist."

"You're so right," she said vehemently. "I made up my mind a long time ago that the man I fall in love with is going to be interested in only one thing: money. I don't care if he doesn't know Shakespeare from second base; just so he knows how to make a buck."

"Can you mean," I asked, aghast, "that you have deliberately set out to marry money?"

"Not at all," she answered. "I'm not looking for a man who's already rich. He can be poor as a churchmouse now, as long as I'm sure he's going to make money later. I don't intend to wind up like my sisters. I'm going to have fine clothes and a big house and servants and everything else."

"Hm," I said, sorely troubled. I was obviously going to get nowhere with this girl. And even if I did, what was there to look forward to? What kind of romance would we

have? What in the world would we talk about? She had
a violent antipathy toward art; I was totally indifferent
to business and finance. Clearly, the wise thing was to let
this affair die aborning.

And yet, looking at the body that encased her grubby
soul, I could not bring myself to let her go. She was simply too beautiful. Come what might, I had to have her.
So I took a deep breath and told a big lie.

"You," I said, "have opened my eyes. From now on I'm
going to think about nothing but making money."

"That's using the old noggin," she said approvingly.

"Would you like to come for a ride in my convertible?"
I said.

Her eyes widened. "You have a convertible?"

"It isn't much really," I said, and really it wasn't. It was
not new nor especially grand, but it was mine and I loved
it. I kept it clean and shiny, and every couple of months
I changed the squirrel tail on the radiator cap.

"I'd love to go for a ride," said Poppy. "But let's
stop at the bookstore first. We have to buy *Snaith's English Usage,* remember?"

I winced at the mention of my tormentor's name, but
the pain quickly vanished. It was impossible to be anything but happy in the presence of the radiant Poppy.
"Come," I cried and, singing all the way, took her to my
convertible.

A short drive brought us to Hammersmith's Bookstore
—New and Used Textbooks Bought and Sold. We went
inside. Mr. Hammersmith glided toward us, rubbing his
pudgy hands in anticipation. "Yes?" he hissed.

"How much is *Snaith's English Usage?*" Poppy asked
loudly. I reddened with embarrassment. I never ask the
prices of things; it has no dignity.

"Four dollars and twenty-five cents," said Mr. Hammersmith.

"Outrageous!" snapped Poppy. "How much is a sec-
ond-hand copy?"

"Three dollars and seventy-five cents."

"Do you mean to tell me," she demanded, "that you only save fifty cents on a secondhand copy?"

"Well, now, little lady," he replied with a storekeeper's chuckle, "that's quite a saving, isn't it?"

"Don't you 'little lady' me," Poppy shot back, prodding his fat chest with her forefinger. He retreated in alarm. "If a student came in here to sell you a secondhand copy of *Snaith's English Usage*," she asked, staying right on top of him, "how much would you pay?"

He looked wildly around for assistance.

"How much?" she repeated and backed him into a corner.

"Two-fifty," he confessed.

"What?" she shrieked. "You make a dollar and a quarter on a secondhand textbook? Why, that's criminal!"

I was writhing with mortification. "Please, Poppy," I begged, "I'll buy the books. Be my guest."

Although she accepted my offer, she was by no means pacified. All the way out to the car she kept muttering darkly. I headed the car for the River Road, hoping that a pastoral setting would dispel her low-grade emotions. She did, indeed, fall quiet as we drove along the steep, tree-covered bluffs of the Mississippi. Far below us the spring-swollen river churned whitely. The day was warm. The air was laden with the sweet scents of earth, newly awakened after the long winter. In the budding trees nesting birds twittered cheerily. The hills were bright with splashes of early wildflowers. I pulled off the road and parked on a high grassy knoll.

Poppy leaned languidly in the corner of the seat, more beautiful in repose than I had ever seen her. A soft, pensive look was on her face. I took her unresisting hand, kissed her finger tips. "A penny for your thoughts," I murmured.

"I'm thinking about the markup on *Snaith's English Usage*," she cried, sitting erect. "Can you imagine that? A dollar and a quarter profit on a secondhand book!"

I stifled a sudden urge to grab her by the leg and throw her down the hill. "Poppy," I said, trying desperately to change the horrid subject, "isn't this a lovely place? See how blue the sky is, how green the grass, how white the clouds, how——"

"Hey!" she cried, thumping my chest. "I got a great idea. Why should the bookstore make all that money on *Snaith's English Usage?* Why shouldn't we?"

"Poppy, the clouds, the grass, the sky——"

"Listen. We could buy secondhand books for two-sixty. That's a dime more than the bookstore pays. We could sell them for three sixty-five, a dime less than the bookstore charges. That would net us a dollar and five cents profit on each book, and we'd be giving the students a better deal than they get at the bookstore."

"Look, Poppy, a bluebird. And over here, a scarlet tanager."

"We'll buy the books at the end of the spring semester. I'll go around and tell the kids to sell them to us, not to the bookstore. Then we'll hold the books over the summer, and next fall we'll sell them to the new freshman class. . . . How many kids take freshman English, do you know, Dobie?"

"No," I said glumly.

"There must be at least three hundred. That means a profit for us of three hundred and fifteen dollars. How do you like them apples, kid?" she asked jovially and jammed her classic elbow into my rib cage.

"Splendid," I mumbled.

"Of course, we're going to need some capital to buy the books. Let's see, three hundred books at two-sixty each is seven hundred and eight bucks. Have you got it, Dobie?"

"Ha," I said.

She ran her hand speculatively over the side of my convertible. "I'll bet you could get eight hundred for this car," she said.

"No!" I shrieked. I would no more sell that car than I would sell a limb. I loved that automobile—loved it, I tell you. "No, no, no," I repeated.

"But why not? Next fall you'll be able to buy a better one."

"I love this car, Poppy. I've washed it and shined it and curried it. I've been *intimate* with it. Can't you understand how I feel?"

"Sentiment," she sneered. "I thought you told me you were going to start thinking about money. Oh well, I should have known. Once a rabbit, always a rabbit. Take me home, Dobie."

One voice within me cried, "Good! Take her home. Be rid of this calculating machine in woman's guise." But another voice cried, "No! Hold her. Retain, at any cost, those chiseled features, those sculptured prominences, those artfully hinged limbs." And the second voice was stronger. I could not say it nay.

"Look, Poppy," I pleaded, "how about if I didn't sell the car? If I just got a loan on it from the finance company?"

"What? And let the carrying charges eat up all our profits? Don't be dull, Dobie."

"I have to sell it, huh?" I asked forlornly.

She nodded.

"All right," I sighed. "But I'll wait awhile. We don't need the money till the end of the semester."

"Don't wait too long," she cautioned. "The market might take a drop."

In the weeks that followed she kept prodding me to find a buyer for my car. I kept putting her off with one evasion or another, but the fact was that I had no intention of looking for a buyer. I just *couldn't*. The thought of parting with that beloved vehicle reduced me to a jelly. The thought of losing Poppy also reduced me to a jelly. I was spending a good part of my time in a jellied state.

And as though I were not having trouble enough with Poppy, a new nightmare came into my life. I refer to *Snaith's English Usage.* Whenever I opened the book, which was daily, I found something new to enrage me. There were literally dozens of rules in the book that were wrong. They were wrong because nobody followed them.

How could a rule remain valid when everybody broke it?
After all, language was not like mathematics, where the
rules were hard and abiding. Language was a dynamic,
living thing. The very essence of English usage was that
the rules had to keep up with the people, not the people
with the rules.

Every day in class I burned with a compulsion to cry
out this glaring truth to old Snaith, but mindful of my
wounds in our first encounter, I held my peace. Only it
was not peace; inside I seethed with anger. For I was one
who loved language much too deeply to stay calm when I
saw it mistreated. Yet what could I do? If I protested to
Snaith again, he would give me the same reply: that his
rules were broken only by louts and vulgarians.

Louts and vulgarians, my foot. My history professor,
a most distinguished scholar, split infinitives every day.
Would Snaith call him a lout? My anthropology professor, who was studded with degrees like a ham with cloves,
used *will* for *shall* and ended sentences with prepositions.
Would Snaith call him a vulgarian? All of my professors,
gentlemen of great culture and learning, broke Snaith's
rules habitually. Would Snaith dismiss all these academi-
cians as fellows of low estate?

One day an idea came to me—a way to confound Snaith,
to repay him for the indignity he had heaped upon me.
I would conduct a poll of fifty-professors at the university. To each one of them I would bring a list of sentences
that were incorrect according to Snaith. I would ask each
professor if he could find anything wrong with the sentences. Naturally, he would not be able to. Then when
my poll was completed, I would stand up in class and
confront Snaith with the results. This time, by George,
he wouldn't blast me into little, writhing pieces. This
time I would do the blasting. "Hot damn!" I cried, smiting my thigh, and raced to tell the news to Poppy.

She heard my tidings without perceptible enthusiasm.
"When," she snarled, "are you going to quit horsing
around and find a buyer for your car?"

"As soon as I finish my poll," I replied, lying in my

teeth. "Right now I've got too much work to do. This is a big job, Poppy."

"All that work," she sneered, "and not a penny richer."

"But it's worth it, Poppy. I'm going to demolish old Snaith. You'll be proud of me, wait and see."

She made an indelicate noise.

Poppy's non-support notwithstanding, I plunged with great zest into my task. First I went through the textbook and selected the following ten sentences which, according to Snaith's obsolete rules, were incorrect:

1. I am anxious to go abroad. (Snaith said you had to use *eager* for *anxious*.)

2. I anticipate trouble. (Snaith said you had to use *expect* for *anticipate*.)

3. I claim that I am taller than he is. (Snaith said you had to use *assert* for *claim*.)

4. I am surprised to see you. (Snaith said you had to use *astonished* for *surprised*.)

5. He was too interested in her to notice me. (Snaith said you had to say "He was too *much* interested . . .")

6. I doubt that it ever happened. (Snaith said you had to use *whether* for *that*.)

7. Under the circumstances I must agree. (Snaith said you had to say *in the circumstances*.)

8. I was oblivious to his presence. (Snaith said you had to use *insensible* for *oblivious*.)

9. The two men greeted each other. (Snaith said you had to say *one another*.)

10. I graduated from high school last year. (Snaith said you had to say "I *was graduated from* high school . . .")

I felt sure that everyone—save Snaith—would agree with me that the ten sentences quoted above were perfectly all right. The poll resoundingly vindicated my conviction. Without exception each of the fifty professors I interviewed found nothing wrong with the list. This was, of course, immensely gratifying to me. Only one thing prevented my joy from being complete—Poppy.

She rode me like a malevolent jockey. "When are you going to finish this stupid poll?" she kept demanding. "When are you going to sell your car? When? When? When?"

"Soon. Soon. Soon," I would answer, hating myself for lying and yet powerless to do otherwise. If I confessed that I was not going to sell the car, she would leave me instantly. That I could not abide. My love for this cash-crazy wretch had grown more strong as her dresses had grown more summery. I knew that inevitably she would learn the truth, but meanwhile I procrastinated and temporized and hoped that some miracle would occur to soften her gnarled little heart.

Between polling the professors and placating Poppy, the weeks sped by at an incredible rate. It was the next-to-the-last day of the semester when I completed my poll. I worked late that night typing up the results. The following day when I came to Professor Snaith's class I was ready.

Poppy was waiting for me. As soon as I sat down, she snatched my lapels in a grip of iron. "Have you sold the car yet?" she barked.

"Ssh," I said for want of a better answer.

"What do you mean—ssh? I've got the books all lined up. This is the last day of school. We need the money today."

"I'll talk to you after class," I said. That's when I would have to tell her the truth; that's when I would get my lumps. But meanwhile I didn't want to think about it. I just wanted to enjoy the hour of triumph that lay ahead. The battle with Snaith was about to begin, and it was a battle that could only end in victory—sweet victory— for me. A delicious little shiver ran up my spine at the thought.

Professor Snaith entered the room, mounted to the lectern. I raised my hand. "Well?" he said curtly.

I stood up. I smiled at him. I turned and smiled at the class. I turned back to the professor. "Sir," I said, loud and clear, "I would like to quote a number of examples of incorrect usage, all of them taken from your textbook." I rattled off the ten sentences. "All of these, according to you, are incorrect."

"Of course," he snapped. "Sit down."

"In a moment, sir, in a moment. I would first like to say that all of the sentences I just quoted are correct."

He started changing color. "Who says so?" he sputtered.

I pulled the list out of my pocket and unfolded it with a flourish. "The following persons: Professor Jason B. Abernathy, B.A., M.A., Ph.D.; Professor Martha Braun, B.A., M.S., L.L.D.; Professor Charles O. Chevins, B.S., J.D., M.D.——" And so on through Professor Erich Zwingli, B.A., M.A., Lit.D.

The class was tittering openly, and I gave them a good-natured wave in acknowledgment. "Well, Professor Snaith," I said, examining my fingernails nonchalantly, "what do you say now?"

"Two things," he thundered. "First, this university is staffed with grammatical idiots. Second, owing to your insufferable insolence, you have just flunked freshman English. . . . Class dismissed."

With a final murderous look at me he swept out of the room.

I felt like a man who has just made a spectacular swan dive into an empty pool. I was mangled, crushed, pulverized. I shambled, unseeing, from the classroom and into the street outside. I was about to be run down by several automobiles when Poppy grabbed my arm and yanked me back. "Why didn't you let them kill me?" I asked reproachfully.

"Come on," she said.

Unfeeling, uncaring, I let myself be dragged away. She took me to my convertible, opened the right-hand door, shoved me in, got behind the wheel herself, and drove off. "We're going to a used-car lot and sell your car," she announced.

"I don't care," I mumbled dully. "Nothing matters any more."

She drove into The Smiling Latvian's used car emporium. The proprietor ran toward us with a cheery Baltic greeting. Poppy waved aside his amenities and proceeded to haggle. I sagged against the cushions, not listening, enveloped in misery. At length Poppy reached an agreement with the amiable Slav. A pen was thrust in my hand and I was told to sign some documents. This I did as if in a dream. Then The Smiling Latvian handed me a sheaf of currency which Poppy immediately appropriated, and we walked away.

"Now we'll get the books," she said, rubbing her hands briskly.

"I'm going home to bed," I muttered and walked off before she could prevent me.

When I dragged my febrile carcass into the men's dormitory, I found Professor Snaith waiting for me in the lobby. I shrank against the wall, my mouth working in terror. What did he want now—to squirt acid in my eyes?

But his expression was friendly, even shyy. He came toward me with his right hand outstretched. "Mr. Gillis, I've come to apologize. I behaved abominably in class today. You were right, of course. You've been right all along."

"Huh?" I squeaked.

He smiled wryly. "I've known it for a long time, but I've just refused to face it. You know, it's a great deal of work to revise a book like mine, and I'm not a young man any longer. I guess that's why I was so upset this morning in class. You proved what I have been dreading for so long: I must revise my book."

"Am I dreaming?" I said in wonder.

"No," he chuckled, "it is I who have been dreaming. The world has passed me by. But you have wakened me, Mr. Gillis, and at last I am going to face reality. I can shirk my task no longer. I'll start work at once. Next fall there will be a revised edition of *Snaith's English Usage*."

"Well," I said, feeling lighter by the second. "Well, well, well."

"I wonder, Mr. Gillis," he said, averting his eyes, "if you would permit me to dedicate the new edition to you?"

"Of course," I replied, giggling wildly. "Sure. You bet. By all means."

"Thank you, Mr. Gillis. You're very kind."

"Nothing," I said with an airy wave of my hand.

"And, of course, you will not flunk English this semester. I am giving you an A."

I remembered that I had not yet shaken his hand. I shook it.

"Goodbye, Mr. Gillis. I hope you'll drop over for tea sometime."

"Love to," I cried, and when he had gone I ran three times around the room. Or perhaps it was thirty-three times. I was much too happy to count.

Then I went out to tell Poppy. Finding her took several hours, but my elation was solid enough to weather the long search. I was still vibrating with joy when I finally came upon her. I seized her in my arms, gave her a thumping kiss, and whirled her high into the air. "Poppy," I declared, "I am the happiest man in the world!"

"You should be," she answered. "You're going to make yourself a nice piece of change. I've got three hundred books all paid for and stored away till next fall."

I made an impatient gesture. "Never mind that. Let me tell you what happened. Professor Snaith apologized to me. He said I was right all the time. He's giving me an A in English. And—get this, Poppy—*he's dedicating the new edition to me!*"

"The what?" she said sharply.

"The new edition," I answered. "Thanks to me, he's going to revise his textbook. There'll be a new edition in the fall."

Her jaw swung open. She turned a grisly off-white.

"Poppy, what is it?" I asked in alarm.

"Dope!" she screamed. "There'll be a new edition in the fall. They won't be using the old one. And we're stuck with three hundred copies!"

I am now a sophomore at the University of Minnesota. I am no longer keeping company with Poppy. Let me emphasize that I bear her no malice. In fact, I have a good deal of admiration for her. It was through her quick thinking that I got my convertible back. She remembered that I was only eighteen and that contracts made by

minors are not binding. If I gave The Smiling Latvian his money back, he was required by law to return my car to me.

Getting the money for The Smiling Latvian proved to be something of a problem, but Poppy solved that too. She sold our three hundred copies of *Snaith's English Usage* to Hammersmith's Bookstore. By making an awful row, she was able to get two-sixty apiece for them instead of two-fifty, so I didn't lose any money on the deal.

Grateful though I was to Poppy when it was all over, I still felt that it would be better to terminate our romance. And to tell the truth, she was pretty sick of me too. We parted good friends. She has since found another swain, this one more to her tastes. He is a chemistry student who is working on a formula to transmute the baser metals into gold.

Nor am I loveless. When the new edition of *Snaith's English Usage* appeared, dedicated to me, I became quite a celebrity among the campus literati. The campus literati, of course, include a number of girls, and they came flocking to me in droves. Girls of this nature, I must admit, are not noted for their physical excellence, but some are less repulsive than others. I picked for myself the least unattractive of the lot—a sensitive young poetess named Lorna McCaslon. We are very happy together. She isn't much to look at, but what a soul! What a soul!

You Think
You Got Trouble?

In 1799 a French archaeologist named Boussard, excavating near Rosetta, a city in Egypt, unearthed a slab of black stone, three and a half feet long and two and a half feet wide, upon which was inscribed a decree in honor of the Pharaoh, Ptolemy Epiphanes. One result of Boussard's discovery was that my father hit me in the eye with a fried egg.

The day I got hit in the eye with a fried egg dawned bright and clear. The sun shone, the sky was blue, the weather was balmy, birds sang. There was nothing in the air to augur an egg in the eye—or any of the other horrible events that befell me on this day. I whistled as I showered and dressed. I picked up my book and, still whistling, went into the kitchen for breakfast.

At the head of the table, refreshing himself with six fried eggs and a tower of toast, sat my father, Herman Gillis. He is a large, hulking man, customarily dressed in corduroy trousers and a leather jacket. His hair is black and abundant. Each eyebrow is the size of a mustache, and his mustache is the size of a beard. His color in repose is that of a polished winesap; when angered he turns the shade of an eggplant.

My mother sat at the foot of the table. In appearance I favor my mother, she being, like me, blond, slender, and fair, though she, of course, is considerably older.

"Good morning, Ma," I said.

"Good morning, Dobie," she replied.

"Good morning, Pa," I said.

"Nyaah," he replied.

I sat down, sipped my orange juice and opened my book on the table beside my plate. For a little while I read silently, then looked up and said, "Patah. Amon. Horus. Kem. Ket. Reshpu. Bes. Ra. Osiris. Sebek."

My father hit me in the eye with a fried egg.

I did not cry out. I merely looked at him reproachfully with one eye while I swabbed the yolk out of the other.

"Herman," said my mother, "you shouldn't have done that."

"Why," said my father, "does he have to go to the university?"

My father does not approve of my going to the university.

"Leave him alone," said my mother.

"Why can't he work in the store?" said my father.

My father would prefer me to work in his store instead of going to the university.

"Eat your eggs," said my mother.

"If he has to go to the university," said my father, "why can't he at least take law or medicine or something that makes a little sense? Why, for God's sake, does he have to take Egyptology?"

My father is at a loss to understand why I major in Egyptology.

"You're shouting," said my mother.

"All right, I won't shout," said my father. "I'll talk nice and quiet. Am I shouting now?"

"No," my mother admitted.

My father laid his hand on my arm—very gently. "Dobie," he said, soft and pleasant, "please tell me why in the hell are you taking Egyptology."

"Pa, I've told you a million times."

"Tell me again. I'm a dumbbell. I'm just an ignorant grocer. Tell me again."

"Very well," I sighed. "Egypt is the cradle of civilization."

"Uh huh," said my father.

"All of our arts and sciences began in Egypt—architecture, sculpture, painting, music, medicine, chemistry—anything you might name. Every pursuit of modern man had it origin in Egypt."

"That's very nice," said my father.

"The history of Egypt is a glorious one, but much of it is still shrouded in mystery. Scholars did not have a key with which to decipher the ancient hieroglyphics until Boussard discovered the Rosetta stone in 1799. Since that time a great deal of work has been done."

"I am thrilled to hear this," said my father.

"But the work is only just beginning. There are still an untold number of papyri to be deciphered, tombs to be opened, pyramids to be explored. And that is why I study Egyptology—because someday I am going to Egypt and make great discoveries and all the scholars in the world will know my name."

"Who," roared my father, pounding the table so hard that all our eggs turned over, "is gonna pay for this trip?"

"Leave him alone," said my mother.

"Sure, leave him alone," replied my father hotly. "Just leave him alone and keep shelling out money."

"I'll pay you back someday," I said.

"How?" he asked. "By making a mummy out of me when I drop dead?"

"That's enough," said my mother. "He's trying to study. You know he's got a final examination this morning."

"That reminds me, Pa," I said. "You'll have to take a streetcar to work. I need the car."

His eyes bulged. Strangling sounds came from his throat. He seemed unable to speak. "What?" he gasped at last. "My new Chevrolet? You want to take a car that I just bought yesterday?"

"Give him the car," said my mother.

"I'll give him a shot in the head!" shouted my father.

"Give him the car," my mother repeated wearily. "Do you want him to be late for his final examination?"

Grumbling, he flung the keys down in front of me. "Listen, King Tut," he said, waving a big, blunt forefinger under my nose, "if I find so much as a scratch on that car, I will pound you into the ground like a tent stake."

"I'll be careful," I promised.

"You better be. And one more thing: as long as you got the car, you can make yourself a little useful. On the way back from school, stop at the commission house and pick up four cases of oranges, size 288, you hear?"

"All right, Pa."

"And watch out you don't scratch the car when you put the oranges in, you hear?"

"Yes, Pa."

He handed me some money for the oranges. "Don't drive fast. Don't park too close to anybody. Don't bring me home a scratched car, you hear?"

"Eat your eggs," said my mother.

"Egyptologist," mumbled my father. "Of all the crazy damn things to be."

"Cheer up," said my mother. "It could be worse."

"What," he demanded, "could be worse than an Egyptologist?"

My mother thought for a minute. "A white slaver," she said triumphantly.

"Bah," snarled my father, and leaving his eggs, he stormed out the back door.

I finished my breakfast and went to my room to study. The scene in the kitchen had left me undisturbed; it was nothing compared to what used to happen. When I first started taking Egyptology, my mother and father *both* threw eggs at me. Now she had finally been won over to my side. It was only a matter of time before he, too, capitulated. In fact, he already had, only he wouldn't admit it. He knew very well that he couldn't talk me out of Egyptology. It was only habit that made him keep trying.

I bore him no malice for his opposition. The poor man simply did not understand. He had worked hard all his life; poured all of his thoughts and energies into his wretched little store. How could he appreciate the glory that was Egypt? My heart went out to him. I longed to take his work-gnarled hand in mine and lead him among the splendors of the Nile—the silent Sphinxes, the brooding pyramids, the magnificent temples that were built when Abraham's people were still a tribe of rude nomads. Someday we would sit, my father and I, and marvel together at an obelisk. It was my fondest hope.

But first, of course, I had to become an Egyptologist, and that took a heap of work and study. My most immediate problem was to pass the examination that would be given at twelve noon. I sat in my room and studied furiously until ten o'clock. Then I got gingerly into my father's new Chevrolet and started for the university.

I had left myself plenty of time for the journey. My house was in Cherokee Heights, a low-rent district on the south side of St. Paul. The University of Minnesota was across the river in Minneapolis. It was an hour's drive, or, driving slowly, an hour and a half. Not wishing my father to pound me into the ground like a tent stake, I intended to drive slowly. I expected to reach the campus at eleven-thirty, a half hour before the time of the examination. Under university rules the doors were locked at the beginning of a final exam and no late-comers were admitted; if you did not get there on time, you simply took a flunk. Only a doctor's excuse or something equally impressive would persuade the authorities to let you take a make-up exam. All this, however, was of no concern to me. I had left myself ample time.

I drove along at precisely twenty-five miles an hour. I kept a safe distance between myself and all other cars. I obeyed all traffic signals. Every cell of my brain was concentrated on driving my father's new car. . . . Well, perhaps not *every* cell. After all, I was on my way to an important exam, and I couldn't put that entirely out of my mind.

So, keeping an alert eye on the road, I ran over a few facts that might come up in the exam. "Aahames founded the Eighteenth Dynasty," I recited to myself. "Nofert-ari was his queen. Their son Amenhotep built the great temple at Thebes. Thutmes I and Thutmes II carried on successful wars against Syria, Mesopotamia, and Babylon. Hashop, the sister of Thutmes II, made a sea voyage to Punt from which she brought back thirty-one incense trees all packed in tubs and ready for replanting in Egyptian soil. . . ." And reciting thus to myself, I ran into a lamppost.

The right front fender folded back in neat pleats. I fought off a wave of faintness. "Don't panic," I told myself. "Don't panic." With admirable calm I surveyed my situation. Obviously the only thing to do was to get the car to a garage and have the fender fixed so that my father would never know about the accident. That meant, of course, that I would have to take a streetcar to the university. It was now a quarter to eleven. A streetcar ride to the university from my present location would take about an hour. I would get to the final exam in plenty of time. There was no cause for alarm.

A half block down the street I spied a garage: FORMAN BROS.—BODY AND FENDER REPAIRS OUR SPECIALTY. Perfect! I drove my father's wounded Chevrolet into the garage.

A small grease-stained man was standing at a workbench poring over a parts catalogue. "How do you do?" I said with a pleasant smile. "I am Dobie Gillis and I have a repair job for you."

"Just a minute," he said, not looking up. He peered closely at the parts catalogue, licked his thumb, turned a page, examined that for a while, licked his thumb again, turned another page.

I glanced nervously at my watch. "Excuse me," I said. I'm in a bit of a hurry."

"Can't you see I'm on the phone?" he replied tartly.

"Sorry," I murmured, noticing for the first time that

an uncradled telephone lay on the bench beside the catalogue.

He picked up the phone. "Sam," he said, "I can't find the number on that sprocket. . . . What? . . . Look under grommets? . . . Okay. Just a minute.

He laid the phone down and started thumbing through the catalogue again. I looked at my watch—eight minutes to eleven. "Could you call him back?" I asked.

"Just a minute," he said. He ran his greasy finger down the page. "Ah," he said. He picked up the phone. "I got it, Sam. Number three-oh-oh-six-eight-nine. . . . No, six-eight-nine. . . . Yeah. . . . How come they list sprockets under grommets? . . . Yeah, it beats hell out of me too. What gets into them guys who write them catalogues? They got rocks in their heads or something?"

"Mister," I said feverishly, "it is no doubt interesting to speculate on the mentality of authors of parts catalogues, but couldn't you do it some other time?"

He waved an impatient hand at me. "Sam," he continued, "I need some bushings. What you got? . . . No, I don't want no more of them Acme bushings. The shims bust off as soon as you scup 'em. . . . All right, never mind the bushings. Send me three dozen head bolts, three-eighths inch. . . . Yeah, and a solenoid for a '36 Olds. Just a minute, I'll get the number."

Perspiration was appearing on my forehead with audible pops. "Mister, please," I begged piteously.

"Just a minute." He riffled the catalogue, found the number, and picked up the phone. "Sam? It's eight-four-oh-three-six-one-nine. . . . Yeah. You got any brazed couplings? . . . Send me three. Now how about a camshaft for a '32 Ford? I'll get the number."

I clutched both his elbows. "Mister," I said desperately, "isn't this the Forman Brothers Garage?"

He nodded.

"Where, for God's sake, is your brother?"

He pointed his thumb toward the front. I looked through the window and saw another small, grease-stained man out by the gasoline pumps filling the tank of a new Cadillac convertible. No help from that quarter.

"Any more brothers?" I asked in a cracking treble.

He shook his head and returned to the telephone. With mounting frenzy I looked at the hands racing around the dial of my watch, while on the phone the Forman brother ordered elbows, bearings, shackles, ducts, tamps, gaskets, sumps, nipples, I-bolts, T-bolts, and S-bolts. My watch stood at one minute past eleven when he finally tired of his conversation and hung up.

I grabbed his sleeve and rushed him to my father's Chevrolet. "Can you," I asked, "fix up this fender so nobody will ever know it's been damaged?"

"Sure."

"Can you have it ready by this afternoon?"

"Sure."

I heaved a mighty sigh of relief. "I'll see you about four o'clock," I said and started for the door.

"That'll be thirty-five bucks," he said. "In advance."

"In advance?" I said, blanching. "Surely we can work out some easy terms."

"In advance," he repeated flatly.

"But I haven't got——" I paused, suddenly remembering the money my father had given me to buy oranges. He would be something less than delighted when I came back without the oranges, but I'd have to worry about that later. Right now the important thing was to get the fender fixed. I peeled off thirty-five dollars, flung it at the Forman brother, and raced for the door.

As I emerged from the garage, a campus-bound streetcar was standing on the corner. "Hey!" I yelled. The streetcar lumbered into motion. "Hey!" I yelled again and rushed forward, breaking every existing sprint record. I was too late.

"Tough luck, kid," said the cop on the corner with a friendly grin.

"Ah, shaddup," I replied.

He grasped his nightstick, and I walked hurriedly away.

I leaned against the gasoline pump in front of Forman Brothers Garage and tried to keep from shrieking. Things were desperate. The time was six minutes after eleven. There wouldn't be another streetcar for at least fifteen minutes, and by then it would be too late. The only solution was to thumb a ride to the campus, but in this case it was hardly feasible. Thumbing rides is against the law in St. Paul. Often the police will turn their backs and let you get away with it, but somehow I felt that the cop on this corner would not be so kindly disposed toward me. He was watching me now with hard suspicion. I knew he would be right at my heels if I tried to move to another corner. I was licked.

A few feet away from me, the second Forman brother was still filling the tank of the Cadillac convertible. A girl sat behind the wheel, drumming her fingers impatiently on the side of the door. Even in my current stricken state I could see that she was a beauty. Under other circumstances I would have hazarded a whistle. Now, of course, I was in no mood. I just leaned against the pump and bit my lip.

"Hey," said the Forman brother to the girl in the car, "do you know that the valve is bent on your left rear tire? Better let me change it."

"I don't have time," she replied. "I have to be in Minneapolis at noon."

My ears sprang up. Life and color returned to me.

"I wouldn't drive on that tire," said the Forman brother. "It could blow any time."

"I'll have to take a chance," she said. "Hurry, please."

I rushed over to her side. "Excuse me, miss," I said, tugging my forelock. "Did I hear you say you had to be in Minneapolis at noon?"

"Well?" she said with no perceptible warmth.

"This is quite a coincidence," I said, giving an enchanting little silver laugh. "I have to be in Minneapolis at noon too—over on the campus. Would you like me to drive over with you?"

"What on earth for?" she asked, looking at me askance.

"Your tire," I said. "In case it blows, I could change it for you."

"Good idea," said the Forman brother. "Them bent valves can go on you any time."

She examined me closely. Her eyes traveled downward from my crew haircut over my honest face, my cheap suit, my neatly polished shoes. "Get in," she said.

"Yes, ma'am!" I cried exultantly and scrambled in beside her. She paid the Forman brother, and we started off.

Now with my great burden removed, I was able to give her a workmanlike appraisal. What I saw pleased me profoundly. I am not so much an Egyptologist that I find beauty only in ruins; this young woman, the very opposite of a ruin, delighted me even more than Cleopatra's Needle.

In age I judged her to be either an early blooming seventeen or a well-preserved eighteen. I being nineteen, either was satisfactory. Her hair was the color that chestnuts long to be. Her eyes were blue, her skin was white, her teeth were whiter. As to her figure, it is difficult to be accurate when a girl is sitting down, but pending a vertical view, I marked it excellent.

"My name is Dobie Gillis," I said with a warm smile.

"How nice for you," she replied.

I waited for her to offer her name; it was not forthcoming. She seemed, in fact, disinclined to talk at all. Shy, I thought, and tried to put her at ease.

"Do you go to the University of Minnesota?" I asked.

"Bryn Mawr," she said.

"Splendid," I said, friendly-like. "And you're home now for Easter vacation?"

"Yes."

"My Easter vacation starts as soon as I finish final exams," I said. "I'm taking my last one today—Egyptology. Are you interested in Egyptology?"

"God, no," she said with feeling.

"You would be," I told her, "if you knew about it. Egypt is the cradle of civilization. All of our arts and sciences began in Egypt—architecture, sculpture, painting——"

"Oh, shut up," she said.

"Very well," I replied coldly and turned away from her. She might be beautiful on the outside, but clearly she lacked the inner fineness that I require of my women. . . . And yet, stealing a glance at her from the corner of my eye, I felt sure that she was not herself this day. Some nervousness, some distress, was upon her. There was a tenseness in the set of her features, in the way her hands gripped the wheel, that bespoke some horrendous ordeal. I longed to lay a gentle hand on her flank and say, "My dear, would you care to tell me what's troubling you?" but prudence forbade.

We reached Snelling Avenue, an outlying shopping section in St. Paul, and the university was only twenty minutes away. I glanced at my watch—eleven-thirty. I would get to my exam in plenty of time. Then suddenly she pointed the car into a parking space and stopped. She got out. "I'll be back in a few minutes," she said.

"Miss," I said uneasily, "please don't be long. If I don't get to my exam by noon, I'll be locked out."

"Don't worry," she snapped. "I'll get you there. I have to be in Minneapolis at noon too, and my appointment is all the way downtown."

She walked off, and I saw that my estimate of her figure had been low. She was richly endowed, this girl. For five pleasant minutes I sat and thought of her contours. As the five minutes lengthened into ten, other thoughts, less warming, came into my mind. It was twenty minutes to twelve. If she returned immediately, I could just barely get to the campus on time. But there was no sign of her.

Another minute passed. My throat grew dry. Another minute. My eyeballs burned. Another minute. Globules of perspiration exploded through every pore. Another minute. Patches of my skin began to twitch, like a horse dislodging flies. Another minute. Passers-by were now pausing to stare at me.

Then she came running up to the car, a shoebox under

her arm. She leaped in, started the motor, and shot into traffic.

"Shoes!" I screamed. "Of all the times to stop and buy shoes! Couldn't you get them later?"

"They're special shoes, and I needed them now. And quit your yapping. I'll get you there on time." She jammed down on the accelerator pedal.

"Shoes," I muttered as we sped wildly down the street. "I may flunk Egyptology on account of a pair of shoes! Never to see the temple at Karnak, the portico of Denderah, the sarcophagi at Assuan, the propylon at Thebes, the grottoes of Silsileh—and all because of a pair of shoes."

"Quit your griping. You'll make it."

We were zooming past Cleveland Avenue, and I brightened a little. The Minneapolis line was only a few minutes away, and the university was not more than three minutes beyond that. The time stood at eight minutes to twelve. She was right; the way she was driving, I would make it.

"I'm sorry, miss," I said sheepishly. "I'm a little upset, that's all."

"Forget it," she answered, not unkindly. "Just keep your eye peeled for cops."

As if on cue, the air was suddenly split with the screech of a siren. I looked through the rear window and saw behind us a white car of the St. Paul police force.

"How far back is he?" she asked.

"Three blocks," I quavered. "Maybe four."

She set her jaw and stamped the accelerator to the floor. "He's a St. Paul cop. If I get across the Minneapolis line, he can't touch me."

I could not bear to watch. I wrapped my arms around my head, drew up my knees, and assumed the fetal position. If ever a man wanted to return to the womb, it was me then.

I don't know how much time elapsed. The next thing I remember is the girl nudging me with her elbow. I opened one eye tentatively. "We made it," she announced, grinning proudly.

I opened the other eye. We were indeed in Minneapolis. The campus was almost in sight. My pent-up breath came rushing out with a great whoosh. I was going to get to my exam on time. After all the sorrow and travail, the despair and despond, I was going to make it. At last my fearful trip was done.

Then the tire blew.

She pulled over to the curb. She looked at me expectantly. I averted my eyes. "Miss," I said in a slow, careful voice, "you must believe me. I despise myself for what I am about to say to you. I loathe myself. I will never forgive myself. This will be on my conscience until the day I die. But I can't help it. I am not going to change your tire."

Her eyes widened in horror. "What?" she gasped.

I nodded sadly. "That's right, miss. I am not going to change your tire. It is now four minutes to twelve. The campus is just over that rise up ahead. I can run there in four minutes. And that is exactly what I am going to do."

"You cad!" she shrieked. "After you promised—after all I did for you—you unspeakable cad!"

"You cannot," I said quietly, "hold a lower opinion of me than I myself hold. . . . And now, goodbye."

At this she burst into a perfect torrent of tears. Now, I am not a man who is reduced to jelly by the sight of a crying woman—that is, if the crying woman is ugly. I can walk through a whole pavilion of ugly crying women without experiencing any feeling except, perhaps, dampness. But the sight of a lovely woman crying is quite another thing. This makes me limp. This destroys my will, my resolution, my very tissue. Even at the movies this is true. When I see Joan Fontaine or Lana Turner in tears, ushers have to be summoned to assist me from my seat. Many theaters in St. Paul do not admit me to sad pictures.

"How can you do this to me?" she wailed, sobbing copiously the while. "You know I'm late now for my appointment. How can you leave me stranded here with a flat tire? After you promised——" The rest was lost in a Niagara of tears.

I tried to harden my heart. I tried to think of the Sphinx at Gizeh, the blue stone of Tafrer, the green stone of Roshata. But it was no use. "All right, miss," I said with a great sigh. "Stop crying. I'll change your tire."

I am told that at the Indianapolis Speedway they have developed a tire-changing technique that is unsurpassed for its rapidity. I feel sure, however, that on this occasion I cut the Indianapolis time by at least half. In a trice I had the spare tire out. In a twinkling I had the car jacked up, the flat off, the spare on, the car jacked down, and the flat put away in the trunk. Then with a curt nod to the spectators who were applauding wildly on the sidewalk, I got back in the car. "Hurry!" I cried frantically.

"Hold on," she warned, and zoomed like a projectile away from the curb. With trepidation I looked at my watch—four minutes after twelve. Too late, too late! But still I clung to a wan hope. Perhaps my watch was fast, perhaps the exam would not begin precisely on time, perhaps they would forget to lock the doors. Meager prospects, all of these, but I had to believe in something or else go mad.

We reached the campus. "Turn right," I ordered. "Then turn left at the first street. Go down to Burton Hall. It's the gray building with the columns."

She careened around one corner and then the other. She pulled up in front of Burton Hall with a horrific screeching of brakes. I vaulted from the car. She sped away. I ran to the door. I seized the knob and wrenched. It did not give. The door was locked.

I wept then. I pressed my fevered face into the fluted surface of a Doric column and let the tears come. I could not do otherwise.

At length the seizure passed. A calm fell over me, a calm induced by the conviction that no more bad luck could touch me. I had suffered all the slings and arrows that outrageous fortune had in its arsenal. Nothing more could possibly happen to me.

Cloaked in this hard-won serenity, I turned my thoughts to the solution of my problem. I had to persuade

Mr. Harrison, my Egyptology professor, to let me take a
make-up exam. This, I recognized, would not be easy.
Mr. Harrison was a typical professor—jaundiced, hungry,
and actively antagonistic toward undergraduates. If I
came to him and recited the events of the morning, he
would not believe me. Nobody would, I had to admit in
all fairness.

If, however, I came to Mr. Harrison with the girl and
she supported my story, then he would have to believe
me. On the strength of her testimony he would have to
let me take a make-up exam. There was only one thing
wrong: I did not know the girl's name. I knew nothing
about her. In all the excitement I had not even thought
to look at her license number. How, then, was I going to
get her to testify for me?

This, indeed, was a dilemma. I sat and pondered. Then
something came to me. Maybe they would know who she
was at Forman Brothers Garage. She might be a regular
customer there.

Across the knoll from Burton Hall was a restaurant. I
walked over there quickly, looked up the Forman Brothers number in the St. Paul directory, and got into the
phone booth. I called the number. "Hello," I said, "is this
the Forman brother who sold some gas to a pretty girl
in a Cadillac convertible with a bent valve in the left
rear tire about an hour ago?"

"Yeah."

"Good! Tell me, do you know the girl's name?"

"Never saw her before in my life."

"Oh. . . . You didn't by any chance happen to notice
her license number, did you?"

"No."

"Oh. . . . Well, thanks a lot."

I got out of the booth and sat down at a table. "Coffee," I told the waitress. I was not despondent. I still felt
confident that something good was going to happen to
me. It had to; I had certainly used up my full quota of
bad luck.

I sipped my coffee thoughtfully. It was clear now that

I would not be able to use the girl as my excuse. My only
salvation was to get a medical excuse. But how? I felt
fine. In spite of all the traumatic experiences I had un-
dergone, my health was never better.

I toyed with the idea of feigning insanity, but soon
gave it up. I knew I'd overdo it. Once you start leaping
about and rolling your eyes, it is difficult to know when
to stop.

No, it had to be something physical. As I looked into
my coffee cup, I was seized with an inspiration. Coffee
speeded up heart action, did it not? I would drink huge
quantities of coffee and then go over to the students' infirmary. When they heard my heart pounding like a run-
away horse, they would surely certify me as unwell, and
I would have a medical excuse for Professor Harrison.

Better still, I would drink all the coffee and then *run*
to the infirmary. I would run as fast as I could. When I
arrived flushed, panting, feverish, my pulses racing, my
heart galloping, there could not be the slightest doubt
that they would give me an excuse. In fact, they might
even write me up for the medical journals.

"Waitress," I cried, "bring me a pot of coffee. Make it
two pots. Quickly!"

The puzzled woman returned directly with two pots of
coffee. She watched with awe as I poured the black,
steaming fluid down my throat. "Two more," I cried,
belching. These I also consumed with dispatch. Full now
to the top of my esophagus, I paid my check and, making sloshing noises, walked from the restaurant.

The infirmary was across the campus, a distance of perhaps a half mile. I got down on one knee, my palms flat
on the ground, sprinter fashion. "On your mark, get set,
GO!" I shouted and streaked away.

I raced pell-mell across the knoll, leaping like a hur-
dler over the students taking their ease on the turf. Past
Burton Hall I ran, past Eddy Hall, past the music building, past the library, past the law school, scattering knots
of pedestrians as a bowling ball scatters tenpins.

As I passed the chemistry building, I thought I heard

the sound of running feet behind me. I cast a quick glance over my shoulder. About twenty feet to the rear, a tall young man was running. His eyes were wild. His coat flapped in the breeze. In his hand he clutched an object that seemed to be a silver loving cup.

Was he after me? I increased my speed. But his long legs soon closed the distance between us. For about three strides we ran side by side. Then he thrust the loving cup into my hand. Having deposited the cup with me, he swerved to his right, cut across the street, and disappeared behind the school of mining and metallurgy.

I ran on, the cup swinging in my hand, utterly confused. Who was he? What was the cup? Why had he given it to me? But these questions would have to wait. The infirmary was just around the corner and a block down the street. I wasn't going to stop now—not after having worked up such a heartbeat and respiration. First I would get my medical excuse, then solve the mystery of the loving cup. I pounded ahead.

I reached the corner, rounded it, and ran smack into a group of about twenty young men all wearing Chi Psi fraternity pins. "There he is!" they shouted as one man.

They then proceeded to hit me with remarkable ferocity. Some hit me on top of the head, some on the nose and eyes, some in the ribs, some in the stomach, some in the kidneys. "Poor loser!" they kept yelling as they clobbered me.

"I am not!" I cried indignantly. It is bad enough to be thrashed for no apparent reason, but to be insulted on top of it is really too much. Poor loser, indeed! I happen to be one of the most sportsmanlike losers in Minnesota. "I happen to be one of the most sportsmanlike losers in Minnesota," I shouted.

Unheeding, they continued to belt me. I was beginning to fear for my life when a cop finally came running up and stopped the carnage. "What's going on here?" he demanded.

"He stole our cup," replied a Chi Psi angrily.

"I did not," I said truthfully. "A guy gave it to me."

"Liar!" hollered one.

"Thief!" hollered another.

"Poor loser!" hollered a third.

"Just a minute, just a minute," said the cop. "Now let's get to the bottom of this. He stole your cup, you say?"

One of the Chi Psis stepped forward. "Yes, sir. We won the cup yesterday in the interfraternity softball tournament. We beat the Sigma Chis for the championship. It was a disputed game. The Sigma Chis claimed that our pitcher was throwing overhand."

"A dirty lie!" chorused the Chi Psis.

"A dirty lie," echoed their spokesman. "We won the cup fair and square. But the Sigma Chis said they were going to steal it. About an hour ago this dirty rat"—he pointed at me—"sneaked into our trophy room and ran off with it."

"This is too ridiculous," I cried, stamping my foot. "In the first place, I am not a Sigma Chi. I don't even belong to a fraternity."

"A barbarian!" they whispered, recoiling from me in horror.

"So why," I continued, "should I steal your cup?"

"The answer to that is obvious," replied the Chi Psi spokesman. "The Sigma Chis paid you to steal it. A barbarian will do anything for money." He turned to the policeman. "Officer, arrest this man."

The cop hesitated. "You really want me to?"

"Yes," they shouted in unison.

"And you'll appear against him?" asked the cop.

Again they thundered affirmation.

The cop shrugged. "Looks like you're pinched, kid," he told me.

"But this is insane," I protested. "Look—they say their cup was stolen an hour ago. I wasn't even on the campus an hour ago. I was on my way from St. Paul with a girl in a Cadillac convertible."

"What was the girl's name?" asked the cop.

He had me there. "I don't rightly know," I confessed.

"Kid," said the cop, "I think you better come downtown."

Panic started to well up within me. "Please," I begged, "please let me go over to the student infirmary. I've got to get a medical excuse for a final I missed this morning."

"You've got an excuse," sneered a Chi Psi. "You were busy stealing our loving cup."

"I didn't steal it," I screamed. My nerves were snapping like overstretched guitar strings. "I was driving from St. Paul with a girl."

"But you can't think of her name," said the cop skeptically. He turned to the Chi Psis. "Watch him while I phone the station." He walked over to a call box on the corner. "This is Mulvaney on the campus," he said. "Send a car to Washington and Fourteenth."

The Chi Psis stood around me in a hostile cordon—not that I needed to be guarded. I couldn't possibly have run away. I was gelatinous with terror. All was lost now. I was a dead pigeon, a gone goose. No medical excuse; a flunk in Egyptology; a conviction for stealing the loving cup; but worst of all, my father was going to learn everything.

I twitched in quick, eccentric spasms. My father: that was the most unkindest cut of all. He was never entirely calm in my presence, but now he would go absolutely berserk. When he heard about the car, the money that should have gone for oranges, the missed final, and the loving cup, he would be transformed into a veritable engine of wrath. Even if I escaped a jail sentence for stealing the loving cup—and that seemed hardly likely—I could not escape my father's punishment. I knew what that would be: life imprisonment in his grocery store. After today's events, my mother's best efforts would not prevent him from yanking me out of college.

A squad car drew up. Mulvaney shoved my twitching frame into the back seat and got in beside me. We started away. My panic mounted with each passing block. It was no small panic, you must understand. It was the large economy-size panic, complete with head noises, icy perspiration, dry mouth, burning eyeballs, knotted stomach, obsessive clutching, spasms in the extremities, and pinwheels around the ears. I had a physical sensation of sanity ebbing away. By the time we got to headquarters, I was ready for the laughing academy. As I saw the cops scattered around the station house, I was possessed by a wildly hysterical notion. Scenes from George Raft movies reeled through my mind—with me as George Raft. I saw myself cringing in the center of a circle of gigantic, bristly-faced cops. I saw bright lights stabbing into my eyes. I felt rubber hoses thudding against my kidneys. "You stole the loving cup," chorused a group of accusing voices. "Didn't you? Didn't you? Didn't you?" And each question was punctuated with a fresh slam in the kidneys. "Yes!" I heard myself screaming. "Yes, I stole it! Don't hit me any more!"

And then a new thought seized me, and my hysteria increased, though it seemed hardly possible. Would the cops be satisfied with only a confession to the loving-cup robbery? Of course not. Seeing what an easy mark they had on their hands, they would haul out every unsolved crime in their files. They would have me confessing to felonies that had baffled the Minneapolis police for years. But that wasn't all. When they had cleaned up the local blotter, they would make me confess to celebrated unsolved crimes in other parts of the nation—the Brinks Express robbery, the Judge Crater disappearance, the Black Tom explosion, the Crédit Mobilier scandal.

A wild, bitter laugh escaped my lips. Only a short time ago I had told myself that no more bad luck could befall me. And now I was facing electrocution in several states.

Mulvaney had me in front of the desk sergeant. "Cossack!" I shrieked. "Beat me all you want. Haul out your rubber hose. Shine your bright lights. Do your utmost. You'll get nothing out of me."

"Calm down," said the sergeant softly. "The only time I handle a rubber hose is when I water my garden in the evening, and there isn't a light in the station brighter than forty watts. You've been seeing too many George Raft movies. . . . What's the charge, Mulvaney?"

"University kid," replied Mulvaney. "Some frat men say he stole their loving cup."

"What's your name and address, son?" asked the sergeant.

I looked up at him. He was a fat, elderly man with a ruddy face and a shock of white hair, but I was not deceived by his appearance. I saw cruelty lurking behind his twinkling blue eyes, savagery masked by his benign dewlaps. "Dobie Gillis, 2897 Cherokee Drive, St. Paul," I muttered.

He made an entry on the pad in front of him. "How old are you, son?"

Son. The fatherly type. The most dangerous of all, according to Krafft-Ebing. "Nineteen," I said through clenched teeth.

"Do you live with your mother and father?"

He wants to know where to ship the body, I thought, quaking. "Yes," I said in a hoarse whisper.

"Be in Municipal Court at ten o'clock Wednesday morning with your mother and father," said the sergeant. "That's all for now, son."

"You mean," I asked incredulously, "that I can go?"

He reached over the desk and rumpled my hair. "You can go," he said, laughing.

Relief flooded over me, washing away my panic—but not entirely. Although it was a comfort to know that the Minneapolis police force was composed of paternal men who watered their lawns in the cool of the evening, there was still the matter of my father to consider. "Listen," I said hopefully, "how would it be if I came to court with just my mother?"

He shook his head. "Mother and father," he said with finality.

"Yes, sir," I said and shambled out of the station. So my father would have to know. Frankly, I would have preferred the rubber hoses. I saw the bleak vista ahead—day upon day in a grocery store, peas and tomatoes, soap flakes and tunafish, clothesline, Vienna sausage, ginger ale, catsup, Fig Newtons, and the pomp of the Pharaohs an ironical memory. And probably a jail sentence too; the Chi Psis had seemed implacable. "Woe," I cried aloud. "Woe and woe."

I walked forlornly down the street. If only I knew the name of the girl in the Cadillac. She could square everything. She was my alibi both for the loving cup and the missed examination. I could bring her to Professor Harrison and get him to let me take a make-up test. I could bring her to the Chi Psis and get them to drop charges against me. The case would never come to court; my father would never know what happened. Everything would be fixed. But who was the girl? Where was she?

I'll tell you where she was. At this moment she was driving down the street about thirty yards in front of me. I leaped into the air with a full-throated cry. There she was! The car, the girl, both unmistakable!

But I was walking and she was driving, and already she was disappearing from my sight. "Follow that car!" I shouted and jumped on the running board of a passing sedan, forgetting in my excitement that they don't put running boards on cars any more.

I picked myself up off the street, bruised but happy. For the impact of my fall had suddenly jarred loose the clue that I had forgotten. I knew now how to find this girl!

I raced into a drug store. I dug in my pocket and pulled out the five dollars that remained of the money my father had given me in the morning. "Change this," I said to the clerk. I took the handful of silver into a phone booth. I dialed long distance. "I want to talk to the registrar of Bryn Mawr College," I told the operator. "That's in Bryn Mawr, Pennsylvania."

There was a short interval while the connection was made. I deposited the $2.80 the operator requested. "Hello," I said. "Is this the registrar of Bryn Mawr College?"

"Yes," said a cultured voice, for at Bryn Mawr even the employees are cultured.

"This is Lieutenant Mulvaney of the St. Paul police department," I said. "We're cracking a big case here, and you can help. I want a list of all Bryn Mawr students who live in St. Paul."

"You cahn't mean," said the registrar, "that a Bryn Mawr gull is involved in a crime?"

"Not at all," I assured her. "We just need her as a witness. Quickly, woman. Innocent lives hang in the balance."

"One moment, please."

I held the phone in my perspiring palm against my perspiring ear. The seconds ticked by.

"Please deposit another two dollars and eighty cents," said the operator.

I looked in my hand. Only two dollars and twenty cents were left. "Just a minute," I told the operator.

I ran out of the phone booth. A little man stood browsing at the bandage counter. "Mister," I cried, tearing off my necktie, "will you give me sixty cents for this necktie?"

"No, thank you," he said politely. "I only wear bow ties."

I seized his little shoulders and shook him violently. "Mister, don't argue," I shouted.

Alarmed, he fished out sixty cents and thrust it at me. I ran back to the booth, flung the money into the slot. "Hello, hello?" I yelled frantically.

"Lieutenant Mulvaney?" said the registrar, "I thought we were cut off."

"No, I had to step out for a minute and arrest a criminal. Have you got that information?"

"We have only one gull from St. Paul," she replied. "A Miss Bonnie Willet, 1734 Bohland Avenue."

"Thank you," I cried exultantly. "There'll be two tickets to the policeman's ball in your morning mail."

I rushed out of the drugstore. I rushed right back in again. I had suddenly remembered that I didn't have carfare to get to St. Paul. The little man still stood at the bandage counter, looking without joy at my necktie. He cowered as I approached him. "You'll need a clasp for that necktie," I said forcefully. I removed my clasp and handed it to him. "That'll be fifty cents."

"Very well," he said, thrusting out his little chin defiantly, "but this is the last of your wardrobe I shall purchase, do you understand?"

"Thanks, pal." I clapped his tiny back, took the money, and ran for a streetcar.

Within an hour I was on Bohland Avenue, a street in Highland Park, St. Paul's swankiest residential section. I walked up the street looking for Bonnie Willet's house. A host of fears were swarming like bees through my mind. What if Bonnie refused to help me? What if she were not home? What if she had left the country? Had I come so far, suffered so much, only to meet defeat?

Then I saw the Cadillac parked in the driveway beside a fine big house. I raced up the walk. I bounded up on the porch. I pointed my finger at the doorbell. "Hey," said a voice.

I turned to my right. There on the porch glider sat Bonnie Willet. There were tears in her eyes, a distraught expression on her face. I did not know what her trouble was, but I felt sure it could not even approximate mine. I ran to her and seized both of her hands in mine. "You've got to help me!" I cried, and the whole hapless story poured from my lips in an anguished torrent.

A calculating look came into her eyes as she listened. "All right," she said when I had finished my grisly recital, "I'll help you if you'll help me."

"Anything," I exclaimed earnestly. "What do you want me to do?"

"Who's out there, dear?" called a voice from within the house.

"It's Bill Johnson, Mother," Bonnie called back.

"Bill Johnson?" I said in bewilderment. "I'm Dobie Gillis."

"You're Bill Johnson," she whispered urgently. "Don't forget it."

"Bring him in, dear," called the voice.

"Yes, Mother," replied Bonnie. She took my arm. "Let me do the talking," she whispered. "Just agree with whatever I say. And remember, you're Bill Johnson."

What now? I thought helplessly, and accompanied her into the house.

It was a house such as I had never been in before. It was rich but not garish, sumptuous yet simple. All the hangings and appointments were stamped with quiet good taste. I do not know of what period the furniture was—my knowledge of periods does not go beyond the Ptolemies; all I know is that the furnishings were uniformly graceful and elegant, that they had been chosen discriminately and arranged tastefully. It was a house where culture dwelt with wealth and breeding with comfort, and I, the grocer's son, was impressed.

"Mother, this is Bill Johnson," said Bonnie.

No casting director could have chosen a mistress for this house more perfectly. Mrs. Willet was the very model of a patrician. From her handsomely coifed gray hair to her custom-shod feet, she practically oozed breeding. Her carriage was erect, her eyes were level, her hands were beautifully kept, her dress was of pastel silk, expensive, severely cut, and adorned only with a small cameo brooch.

"How do you do?" she said. She gave me her cool fingers to squeeze and withdrew them after a proper interval.

"Bill is the boy I was telling you about, Mother," said Bonnie. "He's the one I had lunch with today. Didn't I, Bill?"

"Yes," I said. "Oh yes."

"So you see, Mother," Bonnie continued, "Mrs. Holloway was mistaken."

"Apparently she was," agreed Bonnie's mother.

"Mrs. Holloway is a friend of Mother's," Bonnie explained to me. "She made the most ridiculous mistake this noon. She thought she saw me going into the stage door of the Jollity Theater."

I felt my eyebrows shooting up. The Jollity Theater is a crummy burlesque house on Minneapolis's skid row. It is patronized largely by vagrants, winos, dehorns, grifters, and other such unsanitary persons. What, I wondered, was a high type girl like Bonnie doing in a low type place like that? For I was sure that she had, indeed, been there; otherwise why this fantastic alibi?

"Why, the very idea—me going into the Jollity Theater," scoffed Bonnie. "We were nowhere near the Jollity Theater, were we, Bill?"

"No," I replied with a hollow chuckle. "Why, the very idea!"

"Where *did* you have lunch, Mr. Johnson?" inquired Mrs. Willet.

"At Charlie's," said Bonnie.

"At Charlie's," said I.

"I see," said Mrs. Willet. She pointed to a petit-point love seat. "Sit down, Mr. Johnson, and tell me about yourself. Bonnie has, of course, told me a few things, but I want to hear more."

The heart within me sank. What could I say? If Bonnie had told her nothing about the fictitious Bill Johnson, maybe I could have bluffed it through. But now how could I know whether my lies would check with Bonnie's? I had to change the subject; somehow I had to keep the conversation away from myself until I could gracefully flee this place.

"What a beautiful house!" I said brightly. "May I look around?"

"If you like," said Mrs. Willet. She followed me as I started through the rooms. Behind her came Bonnie, biting her knuckles nervously.

"Charming!" I said, examining an escritoire. "Splendid!" I said, stooping over a coffee table. "Capital!" I said, peering at a credenza. "Jolly!" I said, perusing an ottoman.

"Are you related to the Johnsons on Crocus Hill?" asked Mrs. Willet.

"What a magnificent portrait!" I cried, racing to a painting that hung over the mantel.

"Sir Joshua Reynolds," said Mrs. Willet.

"Excellent likeness," I declared. "Excellent!"

"Sir Joshua Reynolds is the one who painted it," said Mrs. Willet, casting me a curious look.

"I *will* have my little joke," I replied, giggling wildly. "But now I must see the dining room."

I ran into the dining room with Mrs. Willet close at my heels. Bonnie, quite ashen by now, brought up the rear.

"Where did you meet Bonnie, Mr. Johnson?" asked my inquisitor.

"By George, they don't make tables like this any more," I shouted, pounding the fumed oak dining board.

"You haven't answered my questions, Mr. Johnson," said Mrs. Willet, fixing me with two flinty eyes.

"Wow, what a candelabra!" I cried, brandishing it aloft.

"Mr. Johnson——"

"And what is in here?" I asked, springing toward a door.

"Only the kitchen, Mr. Johnson. You can see it some other time."

"But I must see it now," I insisted and flung open the door.

"What a darling sink!" I said desperately as Mrs. Willet closed in on me. "What a fetching drainboard! What a tall refrigerator! What a short wastebasket!"

She had me backed against the electric range now. Her face was hard with suspicion. She reached out and placed one hand on the edge of the electric range to my right, the other to my left, penning me in completely. Short of kneeing her in the stomach, there was no escape for me. "Now, Mr. Johnson," she said in a relentless tone, "you will please answer my questions."

And all of a sudden, like the cavalry arriving in the nick of time to rescue a wagon train from the Indians, there came a knock on the back door. "Groceries!" shouted a voice. The door swung open and a man entered the kitchen.

Mrs. Willet released me and turned to face the newcomer. A sigh of relief started from my lungs. It retreated before it could even reach my trachea. There was no cause for relief. Now I was really cooked. The thin ice was finally broken and the walls were tumbling down and it was Armageddon. For the grocer who had arrived so opportunely was none other than Herman Gillis—my father.

But he had not seen me yet; his attention was on the heavy box of groceries that he was laying on the kitchen table. I grabbed Mrs. Willet by the arm. I clutched her to me and plunged my face into her collarbone for concealment. "Come into the living room," I muttered, dragging her from the kitchen.

"Mr. Johnson!" she screamed in terror. "Mr. Johnson!"

Heedless, I lugged her out of the kitchen, across the dining room, and into the living room, she uttering piercing shrieks and pounding me on both sides of the head.

"Dobie!" roared my father's voice.

I loosed my struggling hostess. Broken and bowed I stood. There was no use fighting any more. This just wasn't my day, that's all.

My father clumped into the living room in his muddy boots. "Dobie, what are you doing here?" he demanded.

"Hello, Pa," I said wanly.

"Where is my car?" he bellowed. "I didn't see my car outside. What happened to my car?"

Bonnie leaned against the mantel, moaning audibly. Mrs. Willet surveyed us in wide-eyed astonishment. "Dobie? Pa?" she said weakly. "What is all this, Mr. Johnson?"

"Mr. Johnson?" yelled my father. "What kind of a Mr. Johnson? This is my kid, lady—Dobie Gillis."

Mrs. Willet staggered to the mantel and joined her daughter in moaning.

My father seized my shirt bosom in his great, hairy hand. "What are you doing here?" he thundered. "What is this Mr. Johnson business? Why aren't you in school?

Where is my car? WHAT HAPPENED TO MY CAR?"

"You lied," said Mrs. Willet to her daughter in a heart-broken whisper. "You lied."

Bonnie stood erect. She set her jaw. Her eyes flashed. "Yes, I lied," she declared stoutly.

"How could you?" whimpered Mrs. Willet. "How *could* you?"

My father stopped shaking me and turned to stare, open-mouthed, at the drama in front of the fireplace. To tell the truth, I was pretty interested myself, in spite of the fact that I had plenty of trouble of my own.

"I'm sorry I lied," said Bonnie, looking unwaveringly at her mother. "I wish I didn't have to. But you just won't understand, Mother."

"But the Jollity Theater!" cried Mrs. Willet distraughtly.

"I know it's a dive," said Bonnie, "but I've got to start somewhere. When I heard they were auditioning chorus girls at noon today, I bought some dancing shoes and went over. And what's more," she added defiantly, "I got a job."

"No!" gasped her mother.

"Yes!" replied Bonnie. "I'm going to be a dancer, Mother. I'm not going back to Bryn Mawr. I don't care if you went to Bryn Mawr and Grandmother went to Bryn Mawr and all the other women in our family went to Bryn Mawr. I don't want to go to Bryn Mawr. I want to be a dancer, and I'm going to be! If you send me back to Bryn Mawr, I'll just run away and get a job dancing someplace. So there!" she concluded and folded her pretty round arms over her pretty round bosom.

Mrs. Willet made her way unsteadily across the room to the petit-point love seat. Carefully she sat down. Valiantly she tried to maintain her composure. But it was too much for her. The tears came cascading down her cheeks. "All the plans I made for you," she sobbed. "Your debut—your graduation—your trip to Europe—all the plans—all the plans——" She threw her hands over her face and cried piteously.

My father patted her clumsily on top of her head. "Don't cry, lady," he murmured. "Don't cry."

Her weeping accelerated.

He lowered his bulk into the love seat beside her. He took her hand and patted it ponderously. There they sat: she the patrician woman clad in silk, alumna of Bryn Mawr, daughter and granddaughter of alumnae of Bryn Mawr; he the gross grocer with a huge, beetling mustache, with muddy boots and leather jacket and corduroy trousers; the two of them hand in hand on an elegant little seat that might have come from Marie Antoinette's play palace at Versailles.

"Listen to me, lady," said my father. "You think you got trouble? Just listen to me. All my life I worked and sweated and slaved—morning till night, day after day, work and sweat and slave. For who, lady? I ask you—for who?"

"For whom, Mr. Gillis?" she said between sobs.

"For him," replied my father with an angry toss of his head in my direction. "For my son. You seen my store, lady. It's a nice little business. I don't get rich, but I don't do bad. And it's all for him. I figured when he grows up he can take over the store and he'll make a good living. But he don't want to be a grocer. You know what he wants to be? An Egyptologist, that's what."

"Not really," said Mrs. Willet with no little amazement.

"Honest to God," he swore, slapping Mrs. Willet on the knee. "An Egyptologist! You ever hear such a crazy thing in your life? All my work, all my hopes—nothing. He won't go in the store. What can I do? Can I tie him to the counter? Can I chain him to the fruit stand? No. I got to let him be an Egyptologist."

"You poor man," said Mrs. Willet, taking her free hand and stroking my father's which, in turn, was stroking hers.

"It's the same with you, lady. You got plans for your girl, you got hopes, but you think she cares? She don't

care. What does she care? She wants to be a dancer. How
you gonna stop her?"

"I don't know," confessed Mrs. Willet mournfully.

"You can't," he said. "I tell you, lady, it's no use. Kids
are all the same—your kids, my kids, everybody's kids.
You work for them, you make plans for them, you hope,
you dream, you pray, and then what happens? They turn
around and do exactly what they wanna."

Mrs. Willet nodded sadly. "Yes," she breathed.

"So what's the answer?" he continued. "The answer is
you're licked. That's all—you're licked. You can't stop
'em. You just gotta let 'em do what they wanna and hope
for the best. You and I, lady, it ain't our world no more.
It's theirs. We've lived our life."

"True, true," she agreed, and then they fell into a long
silence, broken only by an occasional sigh from one or
the other. At length Mrs. Willet stirred. "Goodness!" she
said, dabbing at her eyes with a lace handkerchief. "I've
quite forgotten my manners. Would you like a cup of
tea, Mr. Gillis?"

"Why not?" said my father.

She rose. "Would you children care for something?"
she asked Bonnie and me.

"No, thanks," I replied quickly. I took Bonnie's arm.
"We have to go on an errand, don't we, Bonnie?"

"But there are still several things I don't understand,"
said Mrs. Willet.

"Me, too," cried my father, leaping up. "Number one:
where is my car?"

"No time for explanations now," I called, propelling
Bonnie rapidly toward the door. "Hope you enjoy your
tea."

We bounded across the porch and into the Cadillac
and sped away, leaving our respective parents with their
respective perplexments.

"When you have children," asked Bonnie as we drove
toward the campus, "do you think you'll try to prevent
them from being what they want to be?"

"Certainly not," I replied with vehemence. "Any child

of mine who wants to be an Egyptologist has my blessing —or a dancer," I added hastily.

"That's exactly the way I feel. Honestly, things would be so much pleasanter if parents stopped fighting their children. They never win, and they're such poor losers."

"I'm one of the most sportsmanlike losers in Minnesota," I confessed modestly.

"I'm sure you are," said Bonnie. "You strike me as a very gallant man."

"You are too kind," I protested, reddening.

"Not at all. It was certainly decent of you to try to help me out the way you did."

"Well, it's mighty decent of you to help me out the way you're doing now."

"It's nothing, really. I only wish there was something more I could do for you."

"As a matter of fact, there is."

"Just name it."

"Could you lend me forty dollars? I have to buy some oranges for my father."

"But of course."

"I may not be able to pay you back for some time."

"No hurry."

"You know, you're a very admirable girl."

"Oh, pshaw."

"No, really. You're generous and kind and helpful, and you've got a lot of spunk too. I mean it takes a lot of spunk to be a dancer when your mother wants you to go to Bryn Mawr."

"I think it takes even more spunk to be an Egyptologist when your father wants you to work in a grocery store."

"No question about it; we've both got plenty of spunk."

She drove along spunkily, and I sat and thought some spunky thoughts.

"I sure hope," I said, mustering up all my spunk, "that we see each other again."

"Such things are possible," she replied.

I detected no encouragement in this answer. My spunk

ebbed away. "If you're ever dancing in Egypt," I said lamely, "be sure to look me up."

"Couldn't we," she asked with a maidenly blush, "make it sooner?"

My spunk came running back. "How about tonight?" said I.

"Solid," said she.

I leaned back, tingling pleasantly, and thought, not irrelevantly, what a wise man Shakespeare was. All's well, he said, that ends well.